The
Gentleman
Farmer

Inside Napa Valley:
Ambition, Legacy, and
Harvest of Dreams

Garret Thomas Murphy

Copyright © 2025 by Garret Thomas Murphy

ISBNs-ISBN: 979-8-9995690-2-8 (paperback)

Cover design by Garret Thomas Murphy

Author: Garret Thomas Murphy

The Gentleman Farmer | Inside Napa Valley, ambition, legacy, and harvest of dreams/ First edition

Books are available for bulk orders and book clubs.

Contact your local bookseller or email:

garretmurphy@me.com

Visit: garretmurphy.com

To my wife, Melissa—

a spirit woven of wild herbs and healing light,

tenderness tempered by courage,

sweetness that endures.

She's lived many lives, each truer than the last.

Excerpt from the poem "The road not taken"
by Robert Frost

I shall be telling this with a sigh
Somewhere ages and ages hence:
Two roads diverged in a wood, and I—
I took the one less traveled by,
And that has made all the difference.

Premier

"Embers of Ambition"

The bride's dress seemed to glow as she ran into the vineyard rows, the long satin and silk train dragging dust behind her. She kept glancing over her shoulder, unsure if her fiancé was catching up, her vision narrowed to ten feet by thick smoke. Behind her, the grand modern winery where she'd just been married, along with the newly built barns only months old, were swallowed in an inferno as fierce, whistling winds whipped the flames across the property.

When the sprinkler system inexplicably failed, the fire spread with frightening speed. Guests scattered in every direction. John, the vintner, for some inconceivable reason, plunged into his personal cellar to rescue his most precious magnum of 1923 La Tâche. He was almost through the barn's front door, bottle in hand, a handkerchief pressed tight against his nose, the acrid stench of burning fresh wood, paint, and melting rubber, when a beam aflame gave way and slammed across his shoulder.

Two employees and his friend Finn fought through the smoke to drag him out. Access to the cars was blocked by fire, so they ran through the olive grove and down the road. They somehow escaped, ash streaking their skin, clothes singed, as paramedics treated them beneath a sky of falling embers. In the distance timber crackled and snapped. People ran, some whimpered while some others stayed silent. John could scarcely believe it was all gone. As he sat there, listening to the employees murmuring and to the bride in her once-white dress now blackened with soot, the truth came to him in the haze. The fire might have been sparked by embers from the Argentine barbecues earlier that night — the illicit celebration he had foolishly agreed to host for his friend Mike.

John was a tall, imposing man in his late forties. Elegant and inventive, he was untroubled by doubt and ruthless by nature. He generally pushed boundaries in pursuit of his vision. After years of building a venture that made him a vast fortune, he decided he wanted the kind of life his friend Mike Johnson enjoyed.

Mike was the quieter of the two, sweet-spoken and even-tempered, fair-minded and analytic, yet spirited and just ambitious enough. He had been the CFO of Ai-driv3, the company the two co-founded in the early nineties with a few fellow Harvard bunkmates. What began in John's garage had grown into a global powerhouse, now housed in a smoked-glass sphere towering over downtown Palo Alto—far above local height limits and still tied up in litigation—The company now offered AI-powered data security solutions to Fortune 500 clients.

A few years earlier, Mike had cashed out his shares, much to John's disapproval; he warned Mike he was leaving too soon, and on this occasion John was right, as the company tripled in size not long after. Still, both men had kept a generous stake in lieu of larger salaries, and that cushion bought them freedom. Mike retired at forty-five and bought a property in the heart of Napa Valley. More accurately, he purchased a grand Victorian house that had been gutted and rebuilt with every state-of-the-art amenity, complete with a beautiful pool and sweeping views of the Mayacamas Mountains. His friend David Thompson, a wine writer with the Napa Wine Project who knew a fair amount of local history, mentioned that the land beneath the house might once have been the site of George C. Yount's adobe. Yount, the namesake of Yountville, was the original grantee of the property under General Mariano Vallejo in 1836, something that gave Mike a certain point of pride. As an unexpected bonus, the property also included fifteen acres of Cabernet Franc and Merlot.

From that moment, Mike resolved to release a cuvée of his own, which he christened Bluetooth as a nod to his tech past. Soon after, he introduced another called The General, and you can probably guess where that inspiration came from.

The two friends were, at least in their own minds, genuine wine aficionados. Every third Friday of the month, they gathered with friends for themed tastings, one evening Syrah from the Rhône, another time old Bordeaux or Burgundies. Their unspoken rule endured: outdo the other, no matter the cost. The wine budget soared past reason, and the victor's ritual humiliation of the vanquished—pouring rival bottles down the sink became legend.

Only Mike resisted waste; he mimed the gesture, then drank the second and third-place wines later, savoring them in quiet rebellion. Even though he had vowed to slow down the lavish excess of food and wine, he told himself that a slight buzz was simply the byproduct of his passion for fine wine. Besides, as he'd said more than once, he despised waste above all else—and this, at least, felt justified.

Each man kept an impressive cellar, beautifully designed and brimming with treasures, and the competitive streak between them surfaced in their rivalry over who possessed the most coveted bottles—just as it had in nearly every aspect of their lives since college, expressed through endless, good-natured banter. It was only natural, then, that John, now planning his own early retirement in wine country, intended to design his venture down to the smallest detail.

He was determined to outshine, perhaps even overshadow, his friend Mike, whose modest winery stood in Oak Knoll, Napa Valley. John knew Oak Knoll, at the valley's southern end, was often dismissed as a lesser AVA, cooled by San Pablo Bay's fog and breeze, better suited to Cabernet Franc and Merlot than Cabernet Sauvignon. Yet with global warming threatening vineyards everywhere, he wondered if this region might rise. Mike had warned him that hillside planting faced strict county restrictions meant to prevent erosion and mudslides. But John was the last man on earth to fret over cumbersome ordinances or codes, and he wondered whether fire risk might one day outweigh those concerns, after all, vineyards often served as natural firebreaks. His mind circled restlessly, torn between building in the south or seeking cooler hillside ground.

At last, after due diligence and countless calls, he was rewarded with the name of a well-respected commercial realtor in Napa: Michael Proffitt. Michael and his father practically owned half the city; in Napa Valley, very little seemed to happen without them having a hand or at least a toe in it.

He dialed. "Hi Michael, my name is John Remington. I was referred to you by Becky at the Chamber of Commerce."

Michael replied, "Yes, I know Becky well, she's a sweetheart. In fact, I just had lunch with her yesterday. What's on your mind, son?"

John didn't realize he had reached Michael Profitt Sr., who no longer handled much himself and was known for spinning a good story. His son, who carried the same name, was about to pick up the extension when his father beat him to it. "I'm considering developing a small premium winery in Napa Valley," John said, "and I was hoping you could connect me with the best vineyard expert you know."

Out of nowhere, in response to John's question about vineyards, Michael Sr. explained that in the eighties and nineties only one name mattered if you needed anything in the city of Napa or beyond. The man owned most of downtown and a great deal of vineyard land. He was the overlord, and at times the slumlord, of Napa. Back then the entire downtown was sleepy and rundown. Mr. Taravella rarely invested in improvements; he simply held his properties and let the area quietly decay.

"Thank goodness things have changed," Michael Sr. added. "We are a little more cosmopolitan now, and a lot less Napolitan-mafia."

John was perplexed and replied awkwardly, "Interesting fact, thank you, Michael," while wondering if the Chamber of Commerce had steered him right. Suddenly he heard a click and another, younger voice came on the line.

"Hi John, pardon me, I was on the other line and my father, who founded this company, picked up. Don't mind him, he loves gossiping. Let me know how I can help you."

John said not to worry and repeated his inquiry, adding, "I'm only interested in a very serious project and would like to acquire a significant plot of plantable land, or one already planted, ideally in a well-regarded AVA and, if possible, near a cult winery or another famous vineyard."

"That sounds incredible," Michael said. "I'm going to refer you to Jason, a friend of mine who's a consultant. He's worked with, or has close ties to estates like Bryant, Nine Suns and Colgin on Pritchard Hill, Dana Estate, and Harlan, among others. I'll text you his contact information as soon as we hang up." — "Thank you so much for taking the call," John said. "You've been very helpful. I'll reach out when I'm ready to buy land."

"That would be wonderful," Michael said. "Don't hesitate to call anytime." John hung up with a grin. This felt like a win, and he couldn't wait to get Jason's contact. Unfortunately for Michael Proffitt, loyalty wasn't one of John's strong suits; he'd use him, or any other commercial realtor, as long as they delivered the most desirable plot in Napa Valley.

Deuxième

"Legacy"

Marco is a third-generation farmer in Napa Valley. Plainspoken and unpretentious, he carried the kind of quiet confidence earned through years of honest work. His blue eyes held a glint of mischief and humor, and even dust-covered he carried an easy air of nonchalance. Bald and broad-shouldered, he moved with an energy that seemed endless; making his living from the land kept him honest. He worked hard, laughed easy, and said only what needed saying.

His grandfather, Marco Belladono, an Italian immigrant barely twenty years old, settled near Yountville in 1917 with a small inheritance from an uncle back in the old country. Young but shrewd and resilient, he fought in the First World War and returned with medals to show for his valor. Soon after, he planted vineyards and, during Prohibition, survived by selling grapes to home winemakers across the country. The crates often carried a tongue-in-cheek warning: Do not crush these grapes, place the juice in a container, and store it in a cool place for 21 days, as it may ferment and become wine. The notice was intentionally ironic—a tidy legal cover.

It was said that Marco returned to Europe during the war years. In 1943, he joined the Italian Resistance. His home village of Cassino—where cousins still lived in the stone house where he had grown up—sat directly in the path of the Allied advance north from Naples. German forces were entrenched on one side, anchored around the ancient monastery above the town, with Allied troops pressing from the other, fighting for the road to Rome. Marco aided the Resistance and the Allied effort by disrupting supply routes and making it increasingly difficult for German forces to resupply their front-line troops. The cost was devastating on all sides. When the war finally ended in 1945, Marco made his way back to Napa, hiding a handful of Sangiovese cuttings wrapped in damp cloth, smuggled home as a quiet reminder of the place he called home.

Now, three generations later, Marco, named after both father and grandfather, felt the weight of responsibility to revive the family's farm and vines. Like his grandfather, he knew he had to be resourceful. His first step was to sell part of the land to a hotel developer, who promised, a hotel named in honor of his grandfather. The grand opening of Hotel Belladono was planned for the following year, hopefully it would open in the summer of 2017, near Yountville; ensuring the family legacy would endure. With the profits from that sale, Marco decided a hundred years was delay enough, and with pride, he launched his own wine label: Belladono Cellars.

He struggled at first after his father's death. Most of the vines on the sixty-acre property were far past their prime. Vines older than forty-five years lose vigor and produce roughly half the yield of younger plants—those between seven and fifteen years. Half the tonnage and less balanced fruit meant trouble for the bottom line and long-term viability of his brand.

His father had planted the old-fashioned way—a field blend. Different varieties mixed with little rhyme or reason and no clear demarcation. In this case, three tangled together: An odd blend of Merlot, Sangiovese and Zinfandel. It was a maze only his father truly understood. Now the vineyard had been left to him, a puzzle with no key, no instructions.

Marco had no better options. He had to bite the bullet and call his old high school friend, renowned vineyard manager and "vine whisperer" Jason Moretti. He was proud of his family vineyard, but it looked like a battlefield, hardly worthy of

Jason's time. Yet friendship carried weight; Marco had stood as godfather to Jason's son.

He sighed and made the call. "Jason, hey—it's Marco. Remember me?"

"Marco! Too long," Jason laughed. "Still trying to sort out that vineyard mess your dad left behind?"

"That's exactly why I'm calling," Marco said. "I sold a parcel and soon I'll have a little money to replant. I need your help, and everybody knows you're the best."

"I'm insanely busy this month," Jason said with pride. "And we can't replant until March or April. But how about I come by in two weeks to take a quick look?"

"That would be fantastic. Tuesday, September third—does that work?"

"Perfect. I'll be there at nine a.m."

"Great," Marco said, sounding relieved. "I'm really grateful for any help you can give. See you then."

"You got it. Cheers," said Jason.

He hung up, his pulse quickening. With Jason's help, he could finally replant and restore the family legacy. The Oakville AVA, even the southern end, was renowned for outstanding Cabernet, and his parcel had the right mix of soil and climate, he thought.

And suddenly he could hear his father again, standing in the middle of the vineyard so many harvests ago. Marco had been about the same age then as his son Steve was now, maybe fifteen.

"Son, start over there, beyond the shed, left of the irrigation hub. The Sangio is ready. Start picking."

Marco remembered it vividly. He had no idea where his father wanted him to begin, no idea what he was pointing at, no idea what Merlot or Sangiovese even looked like. So, without asking, he wandered off and began picking the wrong row, the wrong varietal, using the wrong shears. By the time his father noticed, Marco had already filled ten lugs or so.

His mother had brought him a well-earned iced lemonade. She always knew what he liked, Italian mama through and through. Her beef and spinach lasagna was bar none the best he had ever had, even now. She could really cook, and was so loving he recalled fondly.

He was daydreaming, sipping the lemonade, when he heard a muffled sound that slowly sharpened into his name.

"Marco… Marco."

His father handed him the correct shears and said calmly, "You're harvesting the Zinfandel, son, and about two weeks too early." Then he pointed to the next row. "This here, this is the San-giovese. Get to it, please."

Marco held on to those memories. His father had a quiet way of teaching, never once raising his voice.

I wish he were here, he thought. I miss him terribly.

Marco was still apprehensive. The new vineyard depended on the developer deal closing and the funds arriving, and until that happened, the entire project hung in the balance.

Troisième

"The Intern"

Paul Monier, a young Frenchman from Lyon, had traveled to Napa Valley after graduating top of his class at ISARA, a prestigious school of viticulture and oenology. He wanted an internship in California to sharpen his English and gain international experience. Better yet, his uncle Claude had studied in Bordeaux alongside a well-known Napa consultant; the two had even shared a brief stint at Haut-Brion and Petrus. A couple of phone calls were all it took; by late August 2010, Paul was boarding a plane to San Francisco. He was twenty-five.

At the airport, his uncle's friend Jacques was waiting, an unassuming, friendly-looking man with sharp hazel eyes. He looked a little disheveled and unshaven after long hours in the vineyards, but not weathered like a farmer. He was a consultant, after all, and harvest had started early that year. To Paul's surprise, the car was no luxury liner but a metallic-orange Honda Element, caked with mud and etched with scratches, its windows filmed in red dust from countless treks down dirt roads. He would learn Jacques was unpretentious and frugal.

"Welcome to America, Paul! Bienvenue, j'espère que tu as eu un bon voyage?" Jacques said in a thick French accent. Jacques paused and looked up. He had not expected Paul to be so tall, or so fit. At six feet, strong-shouldered and clear-eyed, Paul looked more like a triathlete than a recent graduate. His short hair was neatly groomed, improbably so for someone who had just stepped off an eleven-hour flight.

Paul, eager to show off his English, tried, "Hello Jacques, my voyage was well, thanks you much! Thanks you for picking up! My papa he say hello!"

"T'inquiète, on peut parler français si tu préfères?"

"No thanks you," Paul smiled. "I prefer to learn. Merci."

"Ok, pas de problème. From now on we speak only English," Jacques said. "Saint Helena is about one hour forty-five minutes, so you can sleep if you are tired."

It was his first time in the U.S., and excitement kept him wide awake. As they crossed the Bay Bridge, Paul turned to look back at the sunset behind the cityscape—light pouring into the buildings, shimmering across the water, even giving the bridge's rougher edges a warm copper glow. "C'est Alcatraz there?"

"Oui. We can visit after harvest if you want. And San Francisco, of course."

"That would be super, merci."

He dozed off later and woke just as the last of the golden hour's light faded over Napa Valley's vineyards outside the window. That summer and fall he worked wherever needed—vineyards, winery, even the office. Only a couple of months in did he realize how famous Jacques Rousseau was in this part of the world.

The seasons turned to years. Five years later, Paul stayed in Napa, working with Jacques. He'd risen to Cellar Master and built a strong reputation.

One afternoon, he and his girlfriend Juliet, a beautiful, blue-eyed blonde with a sharp, inquisitive mind he felt lucky to have met and fallen in love with, grabbed a quick bite at Armistice, a local beer hall on Clinton Street with the best-value burger in Napa and a long list of microbrews. Afterward, they wandered toward their car on Main Street. Juliet pointed to a handsome two-story stone building, the kind you might expect in a small French village.

"Isn't that Jacques's friend's place, the one who owns this tasting room?" she asked.

It was Vintner's Collective, recognized by many locals as Napa's first multi-winery tasting room, home to some of the best garagistes in the valley. Roy Estate, one of Jacques's clients, as well as Longfellow, Ellman, Carte Blanche and many others, poured there.

"Yes," Paul said. "That's Finn's place. I wonder if he's here today."

"Let's go in and see," Juliet said, her voice bright with curiosity.

"A little wine tasting never hurt anyone," Paul chuckled.

They climbed the steps, pushed open the glass door, and took in the space. Paul's keen sense of smell registered it first: a faint mustiness, like stepping down into an old wine cellar. Then came the sweeter aromas of wine being poured. It surprised him. This kind of sensory overload was usually reserved for production wineries set among vineyards, not something you expected in the middle of a town like Napa.

That was the charm of a sandstone masonry building older than the Eiffel Tower in Paris. The walls had to be at least two and a half feet thick, he thought, if the scent alone could stir such nostalgia. The sight of the place felt comfortable, like a duvet in winter, yet modern enough to keep you anchored in the present. It was stunning but understated. A glossy walnut bar stretched across the foreground, and behind it rose tall mahogany racks filled with bottles. The room radiated craftsmanship and warmth. Sleek Italian pendants hung overhead, their light spilling across the vertical-grain fir floors, making them glow. Surprisingly elegant for a room decades old.

A booming welcome swept them up. "Welcome to Vintner's Collective, you guys! I'll take care of you right here," said Andy, who ran the bar like his own living room. "Come closer, we don't bite." He laughed, and the two couples already tasting shuffled to make space.

"Thank you," Paul and Juliet said in unison.

"Hi, my name is Paul and this is my girlfriend, Juliet," Paul added. "We're hoping to do a tasting, if possible?"

"Absolutely!" Andy grinned. "How did you hear about us?"

"I work for Jacques Rousseau."

"We love Jacques!" Andy said without missing a beat. "Not long ago, Finn and I were in Bordeaux with him—ten straight days of tastings. I felt like I should've come home with a Master Sommelier title!" He laughed. "Joking aside, welcome, you two."

Paul laughed too. "I heard about that trip from Jacques, he said you were a riot. Is Finn here today?"

"He should be back soon."

Finn often dashed between the tasting room and his new foodie club, Kitchen Collective, a couple of blocks away across Soscol Avenue. The idea came from the Basque Country, where he took his daughters, Manon and Juliette, every year from the time they were five. It was a great way for them to see the world beyond the States, with the added benefit of learning Spanish. In San Sebastián he'd fallen in love with sociedades gastronómicas, culinary clubs with shared commercial kitchens and dining halls. Put on an apron and join in. A home away from home.

"So, what's your preference, white, red, Sauvignon Blanc, Chardonnay, Pinot, or Cab and Cab blends?" Andy asked. "Or maybe you would rather taste Rousseau wines only?" He laughed.

"I drink plenty of those at the winery," Paul smiled. "Let's start with a Sauvignon Blanc if you don't mind Andy—sounds good, right, honey?"

"Sauv Blanc it is. Let's open something we can all enjoy." Andy added a third glass for himself and laughed!

"Perfect," Juliet said. "A lighter white works for me. I'm not tasting much today; I'm the designated driver."

As they began, Juliet noticed a tall, jovial older guy with thick gray hair and glasses, wearing dark jeans and a black T-shirt, come in from the back and greet a man at the far end of the bar. Their banter had the easy cadence of old friends. The other man, a little older with a friendly face and maybe five-eleven or six feet—she couldn't be sure from that distance—spat each pour with gusto, the spit bucket already splashing over its rim. Surely a winemaker, she thought. Who else would waste so much wine? But he had to spit; he'd once drunk to escape, and now Rex tasted with a professional's restraint and intention.

Rex Pickett, as Juliet would soon learn, was the author of Sideways, the cult novel that reshaped Pinot Noir and Santa Barbara's reputation. Everyone remembers Miles's line: "If anyone orders Merlot, I'm leaving. I am not drinking any fucking Merlot!" The irony was that Rex enjoys all wines, Merlot included. And at the film's end, Miles opens his prized bottle: 1961 Château Cheval Blanc, a Saint-Émilion composed largely of Merlot and Cabernet Franc.

"Paul, hey Paul," Juliet whispered, tapping his shoulder. "Could that be Finn over there?"

Paul glanced over. "Yes! That's him."

He knew Finn well from the Rousseau winery; Jacques and Finn were close friends.

"Well, go say hello then," Juliet said.

"In a minute," Paul said. "I don't want to disturb him. Besides, I'm enjoying this Las Bonitas Pinot Noir, I think Finn made this one."

Andy leaned in to greet Finn, whispering something in his ear. Finn looked their way, caught Paul's eye, and raised a hand. "Salut toi!" he called, excusing himself and heading over.

"Comment va, monsieur Paul Monier? Ça fait un bail!" he said—American-born but raised in Paris, fluently French. "And this must be Juliet? "So at last, I meet your better half! Juliet, you should know," Finn said with a playful smile, raising one brow, a sparkle in his blue eyes catching a thin sunbeam through the old windowpane, "Paul was hesitant to bring you to me, worried about how you might react to the dashing Franco-American before you—mid-forties and blessedly immune to time."

"Nice to meet you, Finn," Juliet chuckled.

"I simply didn't want to subject my girlfriend to all your nonsense," Paul said. "She gets enough from the octogenarians at work." Juliet, a well-regarded psychiatrist working at an assisted living facility, laughed gently.

"I got served!" Finn threw his head back. "That was a good one."

"So, what's new at the Rousseaus? Harvest must be close?" he asked.

"Any day now," Paul said. "We're enjoying your Pinot Noir. It's excellent. Where's the vineyard?"

"First off," Finn said, "it's as good as it is because of my friend Don Surh, thirty years' experience, one of the best. Fruit's from a vineyard at nine hundred feet elevation, midway between Sonoma and Petaluma. Cool fog mornings, warm afternoons, perfect for Pinot."

"So what are you two planning this afternoon?"

"Paul has to go back to work, unfortunately," Juliet said.

"Hard work never killed anybody—but why take the chance!" Finn joked, eyes twinkling.

"Damn right," Paul said with a grin. "I just can't wait to start my own label."

"And when you do, I'll help you sell it," Finn said. "Need fruit sources or custom crush, say the word."

The man from the far end of the bar ambled over. "Are you going to introduce me to these young people, Finn?"

"The one and only, the author of Sideways," Finn said. "Rex Pickett, this is Paul and Juliet. Rex is a regular."

"Have you watched the movie?" he added.

"So weird, we just watched it for the second time last week!" Paul said. "Great to meet you, Rex!"

"Did you actually read the novel?" Rex asked, his blue eyes narrowing with curiosity. He had his selling strategy down: start by asking if they'd seen the movie, then follow with, have you read the book? Rex loved the attention — couldn't get enough of people gushing over the famous author, questioning or clarifying parts of the story. There were two sides to him: the celebrated "no fucking Merlot" author, always in demand, and the disillusioned one — the man who still bristled at how he'd always felt treated by studios, agents, and publishers who had undoubtedly made a fortune compared to the deal he'd received.

"Not yet," Juliet said before Paul could answer, "but we promise we will soon."

With a sly sparkle, Rex plucked a copy from the shelf. "I'll sign this if you'd like to read it sooner rather than later."

"Only if you sign it and add a quote for me," Juliet said.

"Let me guess… 'No fucking Merlot?'" Rex smirked.

"Sounds great—yes please, that's perfect!"

Rex was already scribbling before she finished. He paused mid-stroke and launched into his story. "When I wrote this, I was a starving artist, a screenwriter in that shallow pit called Los Angeles. Didn't know a soul. It was brutal. Not until I moved up here to Napa Valley did I find a sense of belonging, a real community, genuine people. I love this place; it's the only wine club I'm a member of. And thank goodness Finn makes a decent Pinot!"

"I'm with you," Paul grinned. "I love that Las Bonitas Pinot."

Rex waved him off and kept rolling. "Oh, and did I mention—I'm a three-time Academy award winner? I won the Oscar for Best Adapted Screenplay for Sideways. Just back from Europe, my play was a huge hit in Latvia…"

Finn, who'd heard the monologue countless times, caught Andy's eye. "I know, I know," Andy said. "I'm not charging them for the tasting. Friends of Jacques are friends of ours."

"Exactly," Finn laughed. "You've worked with me too long, you're finishing my sentences. And please give them a bottle of my Pinot as well."

"Thank you so much, Finn!" Paul and Juliet said together.

Finn hugged Rex and slipped out the back, leaving Rex mid-sentence. "Have I mentioned I also wrote Sideways Burgundy? It starts right here, at Vintner's Collective…

Quatrième

"The Viticulturist"

Jason Moretti was a farmer through and through: solid, grounded, just shy of six feet, broad-shouldered, skin weathered by years beneath the Napa sun. He'd worked under renowned viticulture consultant Oscar Reynada, learning to read vines and coax greatness from soil. Now it was his turn. His reputation was surging, his calendar packed. He shouldn't have been taking on new clients at all. But some opportunities were too tempting.

At the close of his meeting with John Remington, they shook hands, and Jason promised to assemble a team to bring John's vision to life.

This wasn't just a vanity project; the man was serious, and the funding formidable. The first person who came to mind was his old friend Jacques Rousseau. If anyone could shape a dream of that caliber into a bottle, it was Jacques.

Jason stepped away from the growl of a nearby tractor and called. "Jacques, is that you? Sorry, I can't hear anything, I'm near the tractor!"

"Who's this?" Jacques said, half-distracted, the background roar making it hard to hear.

"Guys, guys, get the fuckin' leaves outta that bin, please!" Jason barked over the clamor of harvest in full swing, then cupped the phone. The tractor rumbled forward, dragging a half-ton bin. Pickers darted between rows, dropping to their knees to gather strays, boot-pushing lugs toward the trailer, snipping plump clusters and tossing them in. When the small lugs brimmed, they sprinted to the big bin hitched to the runaway tractor and tipped carefully, making sure no debris or leaves got in.

"It's your buddy, Jason!" he shouted back into the phone.

Jacques laughed. "Ha! Good to hear from you, my friend. What's going on?"

"I need your help with a great project," Jason said, voice raised above the engine. "The guy is well funded and wants to make a serious wine."

"Where is the property, in Napa?"

"That's the thing… he needs your team to find him a property, plant a vineyard—guess I'll be doing that," Jason laughed. "Then we build him a bad-ass winery. What do you think?"

"Sounds great," Jacques said. "Send me his info and I'll call him tomorrow."
"Done! Talk soon, brother."

A sudden rush of pride ran through Jason. He'd worked with Jacques and plenty of other well-known winemakers and vintners across the Valley. He was always confident in these negotiations, but still, he sometimes had to pinch himself. In moments like this, he could hardly believe that a simple farmer from humble beginnings was now working a deal with one of the industry's most respected consultants, Jacques Rousseau — and, better yet, that they'd become good friends.

Jacques slipped the phone away and returned to the rows. He paused deliberately, a moment of quiet contentment, taking inventory of the scene. Even after more than thirty harvests, it never grew dull. It was still something he loved.

The aromas of harvest surrounded him: sweet must, yeast and sugar in the air, damp earth, flinty at times. Some vineyard hands swore they could even smell the leaves and stems as they shifted from green to yellow to burnt orange. Harvest was coming fast on this hillside.

Knowing when to pick for maximum depth of fruit, flavor, and balanced pH was a complex calculation for most winemakers. For Jacques, it was instinctive. Others liked to call him a vine whisperer, though he dismissed the phrase as romantic non-sense. Still, a glance was often enough to tell him whether the vineyard, and Mother Nature with it, was ready to give up its best clusters.

He moved methodically, clipping samples for the lab, tasting a few berries, plucking seeds to study them. He wanted even browning, no green. He chewed the skins to gauge astringency, then studied the foliage, deep green fading to paler shades, yellowing in places. He grasped a trunk with practiced hands and gave it a firm but gentle shake. The clusters loosened and swayed, and in their movement he saw what he was looking for, a subtle signal of when harvest would truly begin.

Jacques returned to the winery around ten. The place was calm; the fruit destined for the Rousseau wines was close in Brix but not quite ready, so the crew was busy prepping equipment rather than hauling grapes. Brix measures the sugar content of grape juice—grams of sugar per 100 grams of solution, with 1° Brix equaling 1% sugar by weight. It's a key indicator of ripeness, though winemakers rely on many other factors before deciding when to pick. Julien Gaillard, his second-in-command, crossed the crush pad with an update. Clients often saw Julien more often, while Jacques preferred to work his magic in the background.

The Pinot Noir from Sunchase Vineyard in Sonoma County was ready, Julien said; harvest would begin in the middle of the night. It was always like this; first fruit usually Sauvignon Blanc, Pinot, or Chardonnay for still wines. For sparkling, Chardonnay might come as early as mid-August at lower Brix to achieve that crisp, bone-dry style. The Atelier wasn't making sparkling—not yet, anyway.

Paul, just back from Vintner's Collective, joined them. "Tout est prêt. Also, Jacques, we just received the new hydraulic press you ordered from Eric Mercier."

The French connection in Napa was alive and well. Eric, Canadian but impeccably French speaking, ran Premier Wine Cask, specializing in high-end cellar equipment and barrels for Napa's top producers. Most wineries relied on bladder presses: reliable, efficient. But the Coquard hydraulic press was different. It pressed in layers slow and even—yielding purer juice. Gentler extraction meant less risk of crushed seeds, fewer bitter phenolics, no harsh tannins. The juice ran clearer, freer, less oxidized.

Jacques smiled. Only the best tools for the masterpieces he had in mind.

"Super, quelle bonne nouvelle!" he said. "Let's move it over by the tanks in the corner. I can't wait to try it. Please make sure it's really clean before we use it."

"Absolutely," Paul replied. "I'll take care of it myself."

As Julien and Jacques walked off in hushed tones, Paul could tell they were deep in planning for the night's pick. That Pinot Noir was destined for an Atelier Rousseau client and would be delivered in the morning to the winery's crush facility in Carneros. Paul wouldn't go—there was too much to handle here. Their own fruit, Sauvignon Blanc from Knights Valley, was expected any day.

At least, that's what Paul thought. But farming always has its surprises.

Cinquième

"Red Earth, Bold Wine"

September third arrived sooner than Marco expected. He spent the morning tidying the vineyard, even though he'd soon rip out every vine. Still, he wanted Jason to see he had the hands and heart of a true farmer—that his family's legacy mattered as much as the flashy projects Jason now oversaw for wealthy outsiders.

He'd just parked the old John Deere 820 in the barn when Jason's truck rolled in at nine on the dot. Marco's father had bought that tractor in the early seventies; green and yellow, narrow-shouldered and stubborn, it ran as smoothly as the day it was new.

"As punctual as ever, thanks for coming," Marco said.

"Wouldn't miss this for the world," Jason said. "Time to put this vineyard out to pasture. Let's finally make a true viticulturist out of you. Honestly, I got worried last year, after you lost all your fucking wine in the earthquake. I thought you were going to give up."

"I didn't lose it all, thank God. Still, 2014 sucked for me. I lost half my barrels and about a third of my wine cases fell from the top of pallets and shattered on impact. That included all my library wines — some that dad made in the sixties. I cleaned up broken glass and wine all night. Even got a nasty cut to make that day worse. See here on my calf, that scar?"

Marco lifted his right pant leg.

Jason winced. "Yeah, that's a nasty one. How the fuck did you manage that?"

"I tripped like a moron and fell on a pile of broken glass. Earned myself a trip to the emergency room."

"Well, lucky for all of us," said Jason, "we made it. The earthquake didn't win this time. Let's get you going with a new vineyard, bud."

"You're the best. I can't wait. First question—can I plant all Cab here?"

Jason crouched, scooped a handful of reddish soil, rubbed it between his fingers the way he'd done a thousand times, then let it sift back. "At first glance, you've got great fucking dirt," he said. "I'll dig pits and run soil analysis to be sure, but at first glance? I don't see why you couldn't plant Cabernet Sauvignon, or just about anything else. This land looks very fertile."

"Music to my ears," Marco said with a grin. "That's what I was hoping to hear."

He hesitated, then laughed. "Remember the old days, before downtown Napa got gentrified? You, me, Joe, Lois, and Brendan hanging at Geezers on Main, where Zuzu is now?"

"Hell yes," Jason said. "Like it was yesterday. Laura and Alex were there too, weren't they? He became a doctor, I think, and he and Laura were dating at the time. I had a huge crush on her." He paused, then added, "And you might be mixing it up—Geezers was where Henry's dive used to be."

"Oh yeah, maybe you're right. And yes, Laura was a hottie, I'll give you that."

"Yeah, she was," Jason replied.

Marco leaned back, squinting, trying to remember. "And if I'm not mistaken, I'm pretty sure Joe and Lois tied the knot a couple years later."

Jason smirked. "Still married, from what I hear."

"By the way, I had you all beat," Jason said.

The old rule at Geezer's was simple: whoever drank enough beers earned a giant glass mug with their names etched on it.

"And whose mug was hanging from the rafters?"

"I know, I know," Marco grinned. "Yours. You were a party animal, and I was a lightweight." "You're still a lightweight," Jason said, laughing. "No partying for me anymore," he added, brushing soil from his palms. "Marriage and too much work have taken the edge off."

His tone shifted. "This isn't going to be cheap, amigo. If we want to do this right, and I know you do—it'll cost money. That said, I've got tricks to save here and there. We're friends, so I'll do what I can to keep it under budget. Speaking of which… Do you actually have one?"

Marco paused, a little skittish. "I made some money from that parcel sale. A developer bought it to build a hotel—they're calling it Belladono, after my family name. Pretty cool, right?" He had good reason to be nervous. The deal was still tied up with the attorneys, and he wasn't sure when or exactly how much he'd receive. Farming was his forte; business wasn't.

"You dog!" Jason grinned. "That's rad, a hotel with your name on it. Seriously impressive."

"Thanks," Marco said, beaming. "As for the budget, I need to keep enough set aside to build up my barn into a little production facility and start my own label… you'll be the driver. I trust you."

"Ok, no worries," Jason said. "We'll get to that later, let's run the analyses first. I've got to run; another rich guy wants a state-of-the-art vineyard on Pritchard Hill."

"Someone's got to do it," Marco smiled. "Might as well be my friend, the famous vineyardist."

Jason hopped into his giant Ford, spun a U-turn, and tore off like a bat out of hell, leaving a thick trail of dust to settle over everything Marco had just cleaned.

"Crazy lunatic," Marco muttered.

His phone rang before the dust settled. "I forgot to ask, are you going to make the wines?" Jason said. "If you want, I can call Bevan. I could ask him if he is looking for new clients."

"Bevan would be fantastic," Marco blurted, then caught himself. "But aren't we a little early? If I plant in the spring, the vines won't bear mature fruit until 2018 at the earliest, right?"

"Yeah you're right," Jason said. "We've got plenty of time."

"Besides, he's not cheap, is he? I might just make the wine myself, and pay him to consult"

"Cheap, he's not," Jason said, laughing. "Gotta run—another call!"

"See ya," Marco replied, all giddy, unaware their next meeting would reveal an unexpected truth.

Sixième

"Roots That Run Deep"

Jacques was having lunch at his favorite Yountville hangout, KOY—a spot where he and Finn often met to catch up. Finn was late again, as usual. After twenty years Jacques was used to it. He ordered a Sauvignon Blanc for himself and a Chimay for Finn, then sank into his phone, replying to the endless emails from winemakers across Napa, Sonoma, and beyond—questions, lab results, crises. Jacques's memory for his clients' wines was photographic: every tank, barrel, vineyard row; what was in each barrel and what had been done to it. Not unusual for him to ask, Have you racked barrel 23 and 44? Get the answer, hang up. Fascinating.

He was still hunched over his phone, texting his friend Ken down in Coombsville. The news was grim—Finn sensed it on his way in. Jacques's face was clouded, attention fixed, the whole exchange ominous.

Finn slid onto the stool beside him. "Salut, Jacques, merci for the Chimay. I needed that."

"De rien," Jacques said, glancing up. "On commande comme d'habitude?"

"Oui, d'accord. What's up? You look serious. Something happen?"

Jacques sighed and set the phone down. "Yes. My friend Ken had an accident, barrels fell from the top of a stack and missed his head by an inch. Still wrecked his shoulder. He had surgery at Queen of the Valley. He's doing better now, but it was close, really close. I was actually in touch with him about using his optical sorter for one of my projects."

Finn frowned, searching his memory. "Who was that again, it's not Ken Bernards, is it?"

"Ken Bernards, yes," Jacques said. "We worked together a million years ago. Now he has his own label, mostly Pinot and Chardonnay. He'll be alright, I think."

"Oh, right," Jacques said, quickly realizing Finn knew him well. "I forgot he works with you down at Vintner's Collective!"

Finn's voice lifted with relief. "Yeah, he's a great guy. I'm so glad he's going to be okay. You know, this reminds me, I need to call him later, find out what actually happened."

You know, it reminds me, did you hear about that cellar intern last year? Doing punch-downs at... what was it? Paso Robles? Maybe Livermore? I can't remember. Anyway, the poor kid was doing punch-downs, fell right into the tank. By the time the crew realized, it was too late. Just tragic."

During red wine fermentation, skins and solids rise to the surface, forming a thick layer called the cap. It can look deceptively solid, as if you could stand on it, but it's only a mass of floating grape matter.

If someone falls into a large tank—often holding several thousand gallons of fermenting juice—it's almost always during a punch-down, the process of pushing the cap back into the liquid to extract color and flavor. Workers use a ten-foot pole with a flat round disk at the end, but one wrong step can send them plunging into the hot, foamy must, often 85 to 95°F and filled with bubbling carbon dioxide. The mixture is thick and disorienting, making escape nearly impossible. Inhaling concentrated CO_2 can render someone unconscious in seconds.

Many winery fatalities have happened this way; even rescuers who jump in after someone often die too, overcome by the same invisible gas.

"He died of CO_2 asphyxiation—terrible way to go."

Jacques nodded. "Yes, I remember. Very sad." He turned and placed a hand on Finn's shoulder. "I told Paul, my cellar guy, to be extra careful after I heard. I've already put in harnesses and extra ventilation at the winery. I'm even thinking about installing a mechanical punch-down system."

He took a sip of wine, paused, and for a moment thought about the effort it had taken to reach this point. The dream had started the day he stepped off the plane from Bordeaux to San Francisco, beginning his climb from cellar rat to one of the most respected winemaking consultants in the country. Even his peers back in France knew his name. And now, against all odds, he'd built his own winery on Silverado Trail. How lucky is that, he thought.

He straightened, a gentler smile easing in. "For now, we'll stick with muscle—and a bit more caution."

Across the room, tucked into a dark corner of the restaurant, John Remington sat in a booth with his very young social media manager. Marie couldn't have been more than mid-twenties. Her hair was a messy, heavily bleached blonde; her green eyes were big and bright beneath too much make-up. She wore a revealing pink outfit that didn't belong anywhere in wine country. She had come straight from San Francisco to meet him for lunch.

They met like this often, either here at KOY or at Lazy Bear down on 19th whenever John was in the city. Lazy Bear was his favorite. It didn't hurt that it was only a few blocks from Marie's home office.

Marie and John had been having an affair for months now. Whether you could call it an affair was debatable, considering her age and his position. Young. Older. Married. Her boss. The power imbalance made the word feel insufficient.

John was pressed tightly against her in the booth, whispering in her ear, kissing her neck, his hands wandering. One of them was buried between her thighs when Marie suddenly stiffened. She had noticed someone standing beside the table. John kept his hand where it was, refusing to look up, almost as if he wanted to see how far he could push the provocation. It thrilled him. He probably hoped for a reaction from both women.

He got one.

A full bucket of ice water crashed over him. The shock rattled the entire booth. Marie shrieked. John shot upright, drenched, sputtering.

A woman's voice exploded across the dining room.

"Asshole! Cheating piece of shit! Mother-fucker!"

Half the restaurant froze. Jacques and Finn both turned toward the noise, though from where they sat, they couldn't see the scene unfolding.

John finally looked up.

His wife stood over him, shaking with rage, phone still in her hand. She had tracked him here with the Apple location app.

"And you," she shouted at Marie, "you're a fucking bitch. Do you have any idea that's my husband you're fucking? Actually, was my husband. You can have him. You look like a goddamn hooker. You two deserve each other."

John opened his mouth but no sound came out.

"You can pick up your shit," she said.

"I don't want to see—" She didn't finish. The manager, bartender, and a waiter rushed in and gently but firmly escorted her out of the restaurant while the entire room watched in stunned silence.

Marie sat frozen, shaking, soaked from the cold water and humiliation. John wiped his face with a napkin, but there was no hiding from the truth: he had undoubtedly set in motion the end of his third marriage.

A few curious eyes were still fixed on them. Women looked disgusted; Men looked quietly glee-ful, even a little proud of him — or so John wanted to believe. The only thing he cared about now was how much this fiasco was going to cost him.

Septième

"Sweet Nectar Of The Gods"

John was hurrying down the pathway behind
Cuvaison Winery when, out of nowhere, a forklift
loaded with barrels startled him and missed by an
inch. He wasn't used to the frantic pace of harvest.
Even before he parked, the air was thick with the
scent of yeast and fermenting grapes. In Napa, that
fragrance meant fall — October and November
filled with the scent of harvest, grounding everyone
in the same sense of place. The winery was crawling
with interns, winemakers, delivery guys, and a
nonstop parade of flatbed trucks hauling half-ton
bins stacked to the brim with juicy grape clusters. It
was astonishing — his first real glimpse of harvest

since deciding to build a winery in Napa Valley. He was here to meet Jason Moretti, the viticulturist he hoped would take on his project and who would eventually become his most trusted ally in Napa.

Jason was at the sorting table with a couple of helpers, working quickly as grape clusters zipped past on the conveyor belt. They had to be sharp-eyed and precise, pulling out leaves and debris before the fruit moved on. Wasps swarmed everywhere, buzzing hungrily around the grapes, ready to claim their share of the loot. Get in their way, these stinkers wouldn't hesitate to be stingers; sting or bite, who knew? Either way, it was painful enough to make the work all the more distracting.

Jason jogged down the steps, larger-than-life energy palpable, and clasped John's hand in a firm shake—true farmer's hands, rough, strong, and still sticky with grape juice. "Welcome to harvest, John," he said loudly. "It's good to finally meet you in person." With a grin, he lifted a glass in his other hand. "Here, taste this, it's my Sauvignon Blanc. Sweet nectar of the gods! There's nothing more satisfying than this moment, after a whole year of work in the vineyards. Everything we've done comes down to this."

He leaned in, lowering his voice just enough to draw John closer. John saw it in his intense gaze—they'd get along just fine. This man was passionate, plain-talking, and relentlessly driven. "I made a couple of calls for you. People I trust completely, winemakers with good, solid reputations. Two are free right now. And between us, the one we really want is Jacques Rousseau. Getting him on our dream team would take this project to another level." He chuckled and said, "Honestly, Andy Erickson, who started at this little unknown winery you may know called Screaming Eagle, would also be a catch. Both can guide you. They've built dozens of top-of-the-line wineries in the valley, they would get you from point A to B in no time. I know a half-dozen other high-profile winemakers, but these two, and especially Rousseau, would be awesome." — "Would you set up a meeting with this Rousseau fellow for me?" John asked. "You bet. Let's aim for late October, if you don't mind," Jason said. "We're in the thick of harvest right now, and I'm sure most of these consultants don't have much time to spare."

"Perfect. In the meantime, I'll call Michael and have him show us a few properties. I heard about one up on Pritchard Hill, it looks spectacular… and not cheap." — "Careful," Jason warned. "Don't buy anything without one of these winemakers taking a look first. They're particular about sites. The right spot or the wrong one can make all the difference. With that said, John, Pritchard Hill is considered the 'Rodeo Drive of Cabernet.' Surely a good place to start."

Jason's words lingered, but John's mind was already miles ahead—on the hill, the view, the dream taking shape. For a man like him, with nearly unlimited wealth, every dream felt attainable, just another task to complete; Mother Nature, however, had other ideas.

Huitième

"John Fucking Rockwell"

Paul parked in the back of the famous Oakville Market, just as he did most mornings around eight. He loved the place, maybe it was the splash of pop art on the south wall, a faded red Coca-Cola sign he always thought was pretty neat.

He strolled inside and greeted Jenny at the coffee counter. She answered with her usual warmth. She was a beautiful, short-haired brunette, a little too cheerful for the hour, he thought. In a soft, sensual tone she said, "Your regular, monsieur Paul? Coffee with two shots of espresso, room for cream?"

"Yes, please," he said, smiling, a little embarrassed. He'd always found her incredibly attractive. Years earlier, before he met Juliet, they'd connected online, exchanged a few messages, and eventually met for a drink. Nothing came of it, though he sometimes wondered if it could have. Still, he'd always suspected Jenny kept a small spark for him, or at least that's how it felt every time he lost himself in her stunning hazel eyes.

And to be honest, even though he loved Juliet more than life itself, he was still a man — prone to his share of stray thoughts and private fantasies. Jenny's body was something else entirely: soft curves, easy confidence, unafraid to flaunt what she had in low-cut shirts and tight jeans. Paul would never cross the line, but he couldn't deny he enjoyed the quiet tension that hung between them.

Out of the corner of his eye, Paul spotted an older gentleman in a crisp linen suit, reminding him of those daily sightings of Mr. Mondavi so many years ago. He used to cross paths with him often while picking up his morning coffee here.

Once, Paul had said, "Bonjour, Mr. Mondavi." Robert looked up, his face lighting with recognition. "It's good to see you, Paul." To be acknowledged by the man who had done more than anyone to put Napa on the world's wine map filled Paul with a quiet pride he still remembered. A wave of gratitude washed over him. Napa Valley was home now, and that still amazed him.

Then his cell phone rang, pulling him back to the present. It was his boss. "Change of plan," Jacques said. "We need to go to Rockwell Winery." It was one of Jacques's custom-crush projects; fruit was coming in from the Sonoma Coast, and Jacques wanted Paul on-site to check quality and tonnage.

"Julien can't make it, so you're in charge," Jacques said. "Check the clusters for me." "Make sure they're not wet, it drizzled last night around Petaluma. No leaves. And this vineyard should average three tons per acre. They harvested three acres for us, blocks 11 and 12. That should give us nine tons of Chardonnay. And don't let it be more than nine tons either."

It didn't happen often, but once in a while, when times were hard and another client had backed out of a grape contract at the last minute, a grower might quietly add extra fruit on top of what each client was supposed to receive. It was a way to avoid being stuck with unsold grapes—passed off as a "bountiful vintage," but Jacques knew better: 2015 had been high quality, yet painfully low in yield. His job was to protect his clients, and their wines, from exactly that kind of trickery.

By the time Paul arrived at Rockwell Winery, the fruit was already there, and luckily, so was the owner. A famous, even notorious vintner, John Fucking Rockwell was an institution. Back in the '70s he was suspected (and, truth be told, often bragged) of smuggling suitcases of prized French clones into the U.S., later building a nursery that propagated and sold superior vines across Napa and beyond.

"Hey Paul, no worries, I checked all the fruit. Just a smidge over nine tons," John called, grinning. He and Jacques were old friends; he knew Jacques's checklist by heart.

"Thank you, Mr. Rockwell, I really appreciate it. I got here as soon as I could!"

"Jesus, call me John," he laughed. "No worries, I've only been running this fucking show for decades. See over there?" He pointed toward the hopper and conveyor belt. "They're already processing the fruit."

"Thanks, John. I'll get over there and help with sorting."

"Bring your cute wife by after harvest," John added. "I'll give her a tour of the caves, an ATV ride through the vineyard, and a little wine tasting. Should be fun! Anyway, I need to grill her to figure out how in the fucking hell you managed to catch that one."

"Lucky, I guess," Paul said with a smile. "She's not my wife, John—not yet."

John chuckled, swirling the free-run juice in his glass. "Well, don't wait too long," he said, lowering his voice as though sharing a secret. "A woman like that doesn't stay on the market forever… and if you hesitate, I might just put in a bid myself."

Paul laughed, shaking his head. "You'd give me a run for my money, John. Better make sure I close the deal first."

John was obviously joking. Besides being more than double her age, he was married to Joy, a wonderful woman he had met back in high school, they were a perfect pair!

John's laugh boomed as he walked away.

Paul's phone rang again. "All good?" Jacques asked.

"Oui. John was here and checked everything out. I'm getting on the sorting table now."

"Oh, super! How's John Fucking Rockwell doing?"

"He looks in a great mood."

"He's always in a great mood," Jacques said. "Glad he checked for us. Then we're all good, Paul. À plus tard!"

"Oui, see you later." Paul had just hung up when suddenly all hell broke loose in the other room, everyone was running in that direction, someone had left the spigot open, while pouring the juice at the top of a large tank. No one noticed since they were all busy receiving fruit. By the time an intern reached the spigot, nearly fifty gallons of vibrant purplish-red juice covered the floor; that's almost twenty cases of wine slowly going down the trench drain.

Paul shouted, "Whose wine is that?" — though he already suspected the answer.

Intern: "Sorry, boss... it's yours. It's the Pinot!"

John Rockwell slowly made his way toward the mess, his cane bending with each stride. He didn't look happy.

"Rookie mistake, Ariana!" he barked. "Now you can clean up this fucking mess."

Ariana, drenched and flushed with shame, was running around with a squeegee, pushing the juice straight into the gutter.

John turned to Paul, disappointment etched across his face. "Well, Paul, you're a smidge under nine tons now. That intern of yours cost you dearly."

Paul couldn't believe his bad luck. He was in a frenzy to clean it up, desperate to erase the mistake forever. There was no way he was going to let

Jacques or Julien hear about it—he wanted to move up in the company, not down. Maybe John Rockwell would get sidetracked by the heavy burden of harvest and forget all about it.

The problem was that John was sharp as a whip and never forgot anything. Let's wait and see, Paul thought.

He didn't have to wait long. The moment he stepped back into Rousseau's lab, everyone was looking at him with the same disappointed expression. He knew the jig was up. He decided to fess up.

He walked over to Julien and said, "J'ai fait une grosse connerie. Je suis désolé, Julien. We left a spigot open during the…"

"I know all about it, Paul," Julien said, cutting him off. "Our client will hear about this, and we may have to issue a credit for the lost juice."

Julien held his gaze. "Next time, go through the checklist. Verify, then triple-check every step your interns perform during harvest and production. You're very lucky. This could have been a lot worse. Now we'll have to wait and see what Jacques says about it."

At that moment, Paul's fate was hanging by a thread, a thin one.

Neuvième

"Dead End"

Marco and his son, barely sixteen, were out in the vineyard, picking Zinfandel near Yountville, sugars at 27 Brix—it had to be today. When both Nextels crackled in unison with an alert from the Napa County Sheriff's office. A suspect in a vineyard shooting was still on the run, somewhere close by, in a vineyard of all places.

Marco was still processing the message when a black SUV tore down the dirt road toward the reservoir. It roared past so fast he barely registered it. Minutes later, two sheriff's cruisers flew in, dust billowing. "Did you see a black SUV go this way, sir?" a deputy shouted.

"Yes!" Marco called back, pointing. "He went that way, less than three minutes ago. I think it was Edward, but I'm not certain. Either way, this road's a dead end."

"Thanks!" The cruiser spun gravel and sped off.

It wasn't until the next day, when an officer took his statement, that Marco learned the truth. The driver had indeed been Edward, a neighboring vintner Marco knew well enough to borrow a tractor from when his own broke down. Edward was gone. He had taken his own life as well as his business partner's, the result of a bitter dispute that ended in murder and suicide, a tragedy that shook the valley.

From that moment, Marco felt grateful he had sold part of his family land to the hotel developer, and he vowed never to take on a partner.

Marco and his son went back to picking. He felt lucky to have access to his friend Dave's winery in Oakville to process the harvest, the same winery where he'd once been an assistant winemaker. Before that, he'd interned and worked his way up to cellar master at the renowned Pyramid Estate, also in Oakville. He knew how to make wine and was determined to teach his son, Steve, every aspect of the business, just as his father and grandfather had done before him.

He'd helped his father farm and make wine since he was twelve. Old-world Italian style was in his bones, it was how he honored the Belladonos who came before him.

He grinned. I need to build the winery, cut the costs. Decision made —he'd skip the consultant and make the wine himself.

When the Zinfandel block was picked clean and piled into half-ton bins, his son had just left for school. Marco rolled up in his beat-up flatbed and stepped into the shed to coax the forklift to life.

Daylight spilled through the doors, no need for the switch. Halfway onto the forklift, something on the seat caught his eye: the jacket Edward had left on a recent visit. He picked it up, thinking he should drop it at the sheriff's office. As he shifted the fabric, his hand brushed something heavy in the right pocket. He fumbled, and drew out a revolver. Shock jolted him. Panic followed: his fingerprints were all over it now.

He tossed the gun onto the workbench. The metallic thud startled him. For a moment he stared, heart pounding, telling himself none of this involved him. Then he shoved the weapon into a drawer, slid it shut, climbed onto the forklift, and loaded the truck.

As he drove toward the winery, bins rattling, he reached it in just under fifteen minutes, a record, he thought, and eased into the loading zone. Through the rust-spotted mirrors he saw a cluster of employees waiting.

Kurtis jogged to the passenger window, grinning. "What's up, Marco? We were starting to wonder if you were even gonna show!"

"Yeah, Kurtis, nice to see you too. I've had a few days, let me tell you. I'll spare you the details."

"Good," Kurtis shot back with a sly grin, half serious, half facetious. "Some of us actually work for a living."

The crew was already unloading the bins and sending them toward the hopper, the conveyor rumbling. He gave the hood a quick double tap. "We got it, Marco."

Marco pulled aside and hurried in. He planted himself by the electronic eye sorter, watching berries race past in a blur, something that always relaxed him. The machine stripped away green berries, shriveled skins, and stray leaves. He leaned over the bin, staring in wonder. There, gleaming under the lights, was a bin halfway filled with berries so perfect it looked like a mound of caviar.

Pride surged. For a moment, he almost forgot the chaos of the past few days and the heavy secret hidden in the shed. One question remained—what was he going to do with that gun?

Dixième

"The Miracle Spring"

Jacques pulled into his friend Ken's winery, a tucked-away property in Coombsville. Beside him walked Francisco, his trusty handyman of more than a decade. Jacques wanted to be sure the sorting machine he was borrowing was in perfect working order, no breakdowns allowed during harvest.

Ken came striding up the driveway from Block 3, a sling cradling his injured arm. It hadn't stopped him from tinkering with a stubborn irrigation line. He was beaming with pride and couldn't wait to show Jacques the new misters he'd installed beneath his Pinot Noir canopy. In Napa, a few degrees of cooling could mean everything.

Experts had warned of longer, hotter growing seasons, and 2015 had proved them right: a warm winter and spring, bursts of searing summer heat, low yields. The misters had given him precious hang time, allowing greater maturity and layered flavor while maintaining balance and freshness. Burgundy in style but with Napa's flavors: great aromatics, a luscious mid-palate, and vibrant acidity with minerality, were always Ken's hallmark.

"Are you sure it's a good idea to be working with that shoulder, your arm still in a sling?" Jacques asked. "Somehow I survived the earthquake last year—barrels flying, hundreds of cases lost, my house chimney down," Ken said. "And now, a year later, in some freak accident, I nearly get killed by a barrel that missed my head by an inch! Go figure."

"I'm just so glad you're okay. Were the racks stacked the wrong way?"

"Nah, on me," Ken said. "I swung the forklift, tried a U-ey, clipped another barrel. It wasn't even full, so it wobbled off, smacked me on the back of the head, banged up my shoulder and arm. One inch the other way and I wouldn't be standing here." Thank goodness his assistant Rory had heard the commotion and came to his rescue.

"Wow… that was close," Jacques said. "You're lucky."

"Lucky's right," Ken grinned. "Another week in this sling and I'm treating myself to my dream Porsche. Life's unpredictable—one second you're on top of the world, the next you're getting crushed by a runaway barrel."

"By the way, thanks again for the sorter," Jacques chuckled. "I'll bring it back tomorrow, promise. Mind if Francisco gives it a look while we hang out?"

"Absolutely," Ken nodded toward the cellar. "Back there, just past the press."

"Gracias, amigo. I know exactly where you keep it," Francisco called as he headed off.

Ken pointed with his good hand. "Yeah, that's it, right back there by the press. Oh, and you've got to see my new micro misters. Had 'em installed this year, and if I can trust these thermostats, they're cooling the grapes a couple degrees during those nasty heat spikes." He watched Jacques, eager for approval.

Jacques crouched under the canopy, examined the mister heads and placement, then straightened. "Nice setup. I hope this works for you. A few of my clients have similar systems and they're happy, their only reservation is the substantial water bill the misters rack up."

Ken jumped in. "You won't believe it, Jacques, but the vineyard was blessed with a surface spring that showed up out of nowhere right after the 2014 earthquake." It sounded almost supernatural, but these odd geological flukes had been reported before in vineyards across California, Oregon, and Washington. Ken had lucked out. The spring tested at ten gallons per minute—enough to irrigate the entire property in half-acre sets. More than that, it gave him extra water for the overhead frost sprinklers he used for early spring protection.

They worked on a simple principle: when water freezes, it releases heat—just enough to keep the vine tissue at thirty-two degrees, even when the air drops lower. As long as the water keeps running, the buds stay protected beneath a thin shell of ice. It always looked dramatic in the morning, the vineyard glittering like glass, but it meant the vines had survived the night.

The newer micro-misters under his Pinot Noir canopy were a different story. Those were for summer, not spring—to cool the fruit, not warm it.

"I've heard of springs appearing out of nowhere, but I've never seen one. How lucky!" Jacques said. "I can't wait to see it. Still, I'm not convinced it's necessary. With careful canopy management, thinning less aggressively, dropping fewer clusters, adding shade cloth, and adjusting irrigation, you can often carry fruit all the way to full maturity while still retaining good acidity. I'm on the fence. But maybe in the future we'll have no choice if climate change gets even more drastic. Who knows, Ken — you might be the smart one here."

It felt as close to approval as Ken would get from Jacques. He let the words settle like a quiet victory. "You never know," Ken said softly.

Onzième

"Red Suede Shoes"

John eased his Maserati into a slow zigzag up the winding curves of Sage Hill; a rise once whispered of Mondavi's legacy. At the summit, a sprawling estate crowned the ridge, belonging to another dreamer: a French vintner with a flair for the theatrical. JPB, as everyone in the valley called him, had opened his doors for a private soirée in honor of his wife, Gia. The guest of honor, Diana Ross, was preparing for an intimate concert against rolling vineyards and a late-summer sky.

Looking across the hillsides, the weight of history and influence was palpable. Between Jean-Pierre Bresson and Gia Carbone—heirs to two of the most powerful wine families, they embodied the artistry of Burgundy and the scale of California winemaking. No wonder they chose to build their home on this hilltop, once synonymous with Mondavi. Napa's past, present, and future seemed to meet here.

John had first met JPB a year earlier at a fundraising gala. They'd playfully battled over an auctioned trip to Bora Bora. The cost hardly mattered, both were deeply committed to the cause; each had family touched by cancer. Raise the paddle high, raise it often. Winning was almost secondary.

At one point John thought, this guy wants it more. Besides, I'd rather win the trip to Paris. With a big laugh, he lowered his paddle and conceded. "You win, congratulations!" he called to his rival to be revealed as Jean-Pierre Bresson as applause erupted.

Minutes later Jean Pierre approached, confessing he'd nearly given up but was relieved to have won, especially since his wife had long dreamed of French Polynesia. With a thick French accent and a mischievous, penetrating look, he leaned in: "I want to show my appreciation and invite you this fall to my house in Napa Valley. It will be an intimate evening, just under a hundred people. I assure you, my guest artist will leave you speechless. One of my all-time favorite singers. The only hint… is Motown."

"Are you French?" John chuckled.

"Oui!" JPB laughed. "Jean-Pierre Bresson, enchanté my friend!."

The name struck a chord. Debonair didn't begin to cover it: red suede loafers, black jeans, a smoking jacket of red and black suede, bold pocket square. The man knew how to make an entrance, John thought.

"I'm grateful for the invitation," John replied. "My wife and I wouldn't miss it. Here's my card. You wouldn't happen to be related to Bresson Estate sparkling wine, would you?"

"That's me," Jean-Pierre grinned. "And this is my beautiful wife, Gia. We'll be celebrating her birthday that evening." He winked. "I think it's her twenty-fifth."

John laughed, shaking Gia's hand. "Pleasure to meet you. We look forward to it. And I hope you enjoy Bora Bora!"

"Speaking of better halves, where is your wife this evening?" Jean-Pierre asked.

John hesitated, softening his voice. The truth—that they were struggling, and she'd chosen Cabo with a friend over this dinner, wasn't something he was willing to share at this moment. "She unfortunately had to travel for work in Asia. But she sends regards to the host, and happy birthday to you, Gia."

"Tell her thank you," Gia giggled, "and that we hope to meet her soon."

Just then someone briskly approached JPB. "Good evening, Jean-Pierre. As usual, this event is grand. I'm so looking forward to hearing Diana Ross in action!"

JPB raised a hand, cutting him off with a quick gesture. "Shhh—remember, Arman, it's a secret!"

"Oops," Arman smiled. "My lips are sealed; mum's the word." And as he drifted away, he whispered with a grin, "I won't say a word!." Arman was one of Napa's most recognizable figures. In the mid-nineties, he built a lavish hilltop estate on Silverado Trail, a nod to his Persian heritage and his success in fashion retail. Elegant, posh, his wines mirrored his taste. Arman himself was soft-spoken and unfailingly kind, with a quiet grace that extended even to the way he dressed.

"I guess the cat is out of the bag," John grinned. "But don't worry, it'll stay between us." Guests began to swarm JPB. With a quick smile and wave, he slipped into the crowd.

The evening was grand: round tables in crisp linens around the pool; white-on-white interiors; extravagant yet tasteful art placed sparingly indoors and across the grounds. Suddenly, just as the guests were about to sit, glasses clinked. To John's surprise, it was the former Speaker herself, petite and poised, pearls gleaming under the light, raising her glass to wish Gia the happiest of birthdays.

She began her remarks; John couldn't have cared less. He'd already decided to vote Republican next time. The front-runner struck him as an idiot, but that hardly mattered. He'd made an enormous fortune and believed voting Republican was the surest way to keep most of it safe from taxation.

He sat and turned to the woman on his left. Sonia introduced herself as COO of Festival Napa Valley, a nonprofit funding arts education, youth programs, and community initiatives. John, always eager to weave himself into the valley's fabric, offered on the spot to sponsor a vineyard concert.

"By the way, do you know Mr. Jon Langford?" Sonia asked, gesturing toward an older gentleman across the table. "Founder of Langford Winery—major supporters."

"Good to meet you, Jon! We share the same name and I love your wine!" John called with a grin. But the room was loud, and Jon Langford looked puzzled. He rose politely, murmured, "Nice to meet you," offered a soft handshake, and returned to his conversation.

"And this is my friend, Finn O' Cleary," Sonia added, "founder of Vintner's Collective downtown, and now the mind behind a new private club in Napa. A club for foodies!"

"That sounds delicious," John said with a grin. "Nice to meet you, Finn. I'm looking forward to visiting."

Finn rose, extending a firm handshake and a broad, genuine smile. "Good to meet you, John."

They clicked immediately, spending the evening deep in conversation about food and wine, paused only when the fabulous Diana Ross took the stage to sing "Endless Love." Not a peep in the room. Her voice filled the space as the indoor pool shimmered, reflections dancing across white walls. Pure magic.

By night's end, John and Finn had plans for a spring visit to Kitchen Collective. What John couldn't foresee was how that visit would change things: he'd meet the people who embodied the valley—some actual rock stars in the wine industry, others who would grow into some of his closest friends.

Douzième

"Sabrage gone wrong"

Paul was setting the table under Juliet's watchful eye. "Seven, not six, Paul. I also invited Julien from work; his wife couldn't make it."

But Paul's eyes were locked on the TV: his team, Les Rouges, in a nail-biting penalty shootout. Keeper Baptiste Reynet was pulling off the impossible. "Paul, are you listening?" Juliet snapped. "We're starting with charcuterie from Fatted Calf, and I picked up cheese at Sunshine. Add small plates, please." He blinked back to the room, switched off the TV, and resumed his task. "Oui, chérie, I heard you." Then, with a grin: "Did you pick up some Brie de Meaux?"

"Yes," Juliet replied dryly. "And it's a stinker."

"Pairs perfectly with my mouth," Paul said, smiling. "And that's exactly why I won't be kissing that mouth tonight!" Juliet smirked.

They felt fortunate to have found their little house with a yard in St. Helena, just off Spring Street, a posh neighborhood with wonderful neighbors. That evening, the Carpenters were joining them. Juliet especially enjoyed Tina, whose bubbly personality lit a room. Her husband Chris, the broad-shouldered winemaker of Cardinale, wore his thick mustache like a badge of honor. Older, yes, but endlessly fun. Juliet hoped Tina might bring a bottle of her own sparkling project, Pink Girl Wines.

Paul's friend Vincent Garry was coming with his girlfriend. A big name at Ermitage, the renowned French cooperage, Vincent split time between the U.S. and his home near Bordeaux. Paul used Ermitage barrels at Rousseau Estate and admired them. He and Vincent had clicked: both soft-spoken, witty, and impeccably dressed. Paul was sure he'd get along famously with the Carpenters.

Dinner began with Paul attempting sabrage. Vincent, true to form, had brought something spectacular: a 2008 Jacques Selosse, an obscure grower Champagne elevated to cult status. Parker had even given it 100 points. Everyone was eager to taste it.

Paul had sabered bottles his whole life. But tonight, knowing this one was rare and priceless, he held back, choosing a careful motion beneath the lip. Nothing. Laughter. A second cautious attempt. Still nothing. Laughter louder.

Enough. He raised the blade and brought it down hard. A crack. Silence. The bottle exploded in his hand, leaving only a jagged stump of glass.

The room froze. Eyes widened. Vincent looked distressed. Paul turned beet red, then glanced at the remains and, with forced cheer, exclaimed, "Well—lucky for us, there's still enough left to taste!"

Tension broke. Glasses shot forward in unison, no one caring if shards had slipped into the pour. They drank, they laughed, and a $4,000 disaster became an unforgettable memory.

Later, over the last sips, Julien grew a little tipsy, though it was hardly noticeable. He was a good-looking guy with a big wave of long dark hair that made him look like a mad scientist, a stocky winemaker who could usually hold his liquor. Most winemakers are practically drunk-proof, and Julien was no exception. His friendly, playful demeanor, combined with a strong French accent, meant that most of what he said sounded like gentle mumbling anyway. You could barely tell the difference between tipsy and sober with him.

He leaned in and confided that he was leaving Rousseau Estate to pursue his own project. An investor had backed him, and together they were planning a new Coombsville winery not far from Rockwell Estate. For the first time, Paul admitted to Julien, and to himself, that he too dreamed of creating his own label.

"Good idea, Paul," Julien said. "Because next time, Jacques might not be so forgiving if you fuck up. That Rockwell incident cost him a few bucks, and you know how he is. He'd bend down to pick up a penny." He chuckled. "Even now, with pennies on their way out."

Then he softened. "But joking aside, when you're ready," he said with a smile, "I'll give you a corner of my winery to make your first batch."

Paul had barely begun to thank him when Vincent chimed in, shouting in French, "Tu auras besoin de quelques bonnes barriques. Ce sera mon cadeau!" You'll need some good barrels. That'll be my gift.

Paul blinked. Free French oak at nearly a thousand dollars a barrel was no small offer. For the first time, his dream felt within reach. He would start small, perhaps a rosé or a Pinot Noir, something that wouldn't compete with the Bordeaux blends at Atelier Rousseau. Then, with luck, and maybe a bit of backing, he could one day build his own winery and plant his own vineyard. Paul took another sip, a spark of self-belief rising inside him. Maybe, for once, the small guy gets a win. If Julien could do it, why not him?

Treizième

"The Flavor of Belonging"

When John arrived at Kitchen Collective in March 2017, the place was alive with energy. The grand atrium gleamed, surrounded by massive sliding doors on all sides. In the center, a roaring fireplace blazed upward, its flames reaching toward the open sky, surrounded by beautiful Japanese maple trees whose delicate crimson leaves glowed in the firelight.

Through the tall glass doors to the east, John noticed a small, cozy living room, elegantly appointed, complete with its own crackling fireplace. Inside, he immediately recognized Carlo

Mondavi. They had met once before at an equipment show in Sacramento, where both had been drawn to the new wave of zero-emission, battery-powered tractors. John admired the Monarch for its silence and efficiency; Carlo, ever the idealist, wanted to save the planet and run his vineyards sustainably.

Carlo was laughing now, showing a woman how to pop a bottle of champagne with a saber. She might have been the singer-songwriter Skylar Grey; blonde ponytail, a smile caught between excitement and fear, the unmistakable tattoo across her chest that read Woodrat. John remembered seeing her once before at a private event, his daughter having been a big fan. They stood beside an enormous flat-screen TV, cleverly recessed into a towering bookshelf.

The open kitchen buzzed with chefs and guests cooking side by side, glasses clinking, laughter rising over the sound of sizzling pans. The air was rich with the heady aroma of Moroccan and Indian spices. To the west, the dining room was full of guests; to the south, the bar beckoned, its wide doors flung open as a jazz quartet tore through a tune like it was their final set of the night.

Just then, Finn approached with a wide grin. He wore his usual dark jeans but had dressed them up with a crisp shirt and a tailored sport coat, he looked dapper, confident. Then again, everyone in this club looked like a million dollars.

Finn greeted him warmly. "What a wonderful surprise, John! I thought you weren't going to make it today."

"With this crazy winery build I'm attempting, it's never a boring day," John laughed. "That roof—undulating above me like a wave of concrete and titanium, it's beautiful, yet perpetually on the verge of falling."

Finn chuckled. "Well, hopefully it's not really falling, John."

"No it's not," John said, grinning. "But it's nerve-racking all the same."

"John, let me introduce you to some of my friends who are cooking in the kitchen," Finn said, motioning toward the bustle of chefs and guests. "I suspect that's your favorite corner of the club—I know you love to cook!"

They started walking toward the open kitchen when a club member stepped into their path.

"Hi Finn! These musicians are incredible, we've got to bring them back soon."

"We are, Peter," Finn replied with a grin. "They're already lined up for our Sunday brunch next month." Then, turning to John, he added, "By the way, John, this is Peter Johansen, the farmer behind The French Laundry's garden and one of the most inventive growers in the valley."

Peter extended a hand, his smile quick and genuine, the kind that came from years spent outdoors. "Nice to meet you, John. Finn told me about your winery project. Sounds like quite an adventure."

"Likewise," John said, shaking his hand. "I've heard your name more than once whispered in kitchens from here to New York. They say you grow flavor itself."

Peter chuckled, a modest shrug softening the praise. "I just listen to what the plants want," he murmured.

Just then, a cheerful voice carried across the patio. "Peter! Where's my Manhattan?"

It was his wife, Gwen, calling from a table near the outdoor fireplace, her smile wide and teasing beneath the soft glow of the flames. Peter glanced down at his hands, two coupe glasses, one garnished with a soaked cherry, and laughed at his own distraction.

"Ah, caught red-handed," he said with a quick grin. With a polite nod to John and Finn, he excused himself and crossed the patio to deliver the long-awaited cocktail.

As they stepped into the kitchen, the aromas became overwhelmingly enticing, spices, citrus, and slow-simmering meat blending into a mouthwatering perfume.

"Hi, Finn!" a cheerful voice called out. "Try my lamb tagine! I hope you don't mind, we're using the blue swirly one that was on display?"

It was Stacy, ladle in hand and eyes gleaming.

"Hi, Stacy, no worries" Finn replied, inhaling deeply. "It smells heavenly, I'm sure it's—"

Before he could finish, Stacy interrupted with a laugh, thrusting a wooden spoon straight into his mouth.

"Oh my God," Finn managed between bites, "this is your best so far. These flavors are amazing! Nice work—and compliments to Chef Antonia, wherever she's hiding."

Stacy grinned. "She's not hiding, she's delivering the feast to my table in the dining room. You should join us when you have a minute. Brian Nuss is here, telling me all about his trip to Morocco with his friend Robin Williams. He said he brought you back a djellaba!" Brian had been friends with the comedian for decades and had even built his home in Napa Valley.

"I want to see you wear that the next time we have a themed party!" she burst out laughing.

"I'm not afraid," replied Finn, with a wide grin.

Chef Antonia was one of the club's resident chefs, known for her generous spirit and fearless blends of flavor. Her specialties ranged from the soul of Louisiana's classics, jambalaya and crawfish boil, typically served in late spring, to the exotic warmth of Moroccan and Spanish dishes, like the tagine simmering before them that night.

"John, meet Stacy—she and her husband Adam own this fabulous winery here in Napa," Finn said. "You'll discover very quickly they're among the sweetest people in the valley."

Finn hadn't even finished the introduction when Stacy reached for a glass, poured a splash of red from a nearby bottle, and handed it to John.

"This is our Cabernet Sauvignon from Oak Knoll," she said proudly. "We're very fond of this one."

John accepted the glass with a smile. "That's so kind of you, Stacy. I'm looking forward to getting to know you and your husband, uh…"

"Speaking of Adam," she interrupted playfully, "he's probably wondering where I've disappeared to."

John took a sip and nodded approvingly. "This is a delicious Cab, Stacy."

She smiled, thanked him, then lifted a dish from the counter. "Hope you join our KC family, John!" she called out with a bright laugh as she disappeared toward the dining room.

Next, Finn and John made their way slowly to the bar. Everyone seemed eager to meet John; in the span of a few introductions, he felt as though he'd found a circle of food lovers much like himself.

They finally took their seats at the bar, and John, unable to contain his excitement, turned to Finn.

"Finn, you've got yourself a new member! This place is magic, I'm going to enjoy it thoroughly. Being somewhat new to Napa, I have a feeling I'm going to make plenty of new friends here."

Tim Bacino, a surprisingly seventh-genera-tion vintner, and his fittingly named wine, Gen 7, were part of the evening's company. Beside him sat

Will Marcencia, the gregarious owner of the local radio station The Vine. As usual, the two were laughing out loud, trading jokes with the club's general manager.

"Marsha… Marsha," Will called out with a grin. "Why did the grape stop in the middle of the road?"

Marsha barely had time to roll her eyes before Will delivered the punch line himself.

"It ran out of juice!"

He quickly fired another.

"At Kitchen Collective, new members are encouraged to mingle. So far, everyone's doing great, except the introverts, who've formed a very exclusive sub-club called; The Waiting List."

Laughter burst from the bar, echoing through the atrium. Will almost fell off his stool.

Marsha replied with a smile. "That one was better, Will."

Then, as the jazz swelled, it began to drown out the chatter. John felt content, at peace. All the stress he'd carried from construction mishaps, permit delays, and mounting costs seemed to dissolve into the sound. He leaned back, a faint smile tugging at his lips, the music melting the night into something easy, something that, for the first time in a long while, felt like home.

Quatorzième

"Kissing the Pallino"

John and Mike faced off on the public bocce courts at Crane Park in St. Helena, the air buzzing. Rivals for years, they were finally in the league final. John's team, Boccelaw, hadn't lost a tournament since 2015—four straight years. Mike, captain of the Hotshots, a name he thought had just the right edge, intended to end the streak.

Most everyone was still wearing their covid mask, though John thought it unnecessary in the open air. Unlike Mike, who trusted the experts with steady conviction, John carried his doubts like armor. His mask dangled loose, more a gesture of politeness than belief. To him, the world reeked of theater, scientists reciting lines, neighbors obsessively wiping down everything, even their grocery bags, with alcohol wipes. And in his sly smile lingered the pride of a man convinced he'd seen through the charade.

"So, how's the winery coming along?" Mike asked. "Did you finally get those permits?"

"The county's being impossible," John said, "but my lawsuit with the neighbors is looking good. Tod's shredding this guy in court; I should be able to break ground soon."

"Yeah, the county made my life hell too," Mike said.

"They have already delayed my winery at least by three years," John replied.

"Pritchard Hill's the best dirt in Napa," John continued with a smirk. "Martenas sits just below Houyi, not far from Chappellet and Ovid, but you'd think I was planting on sacred ground the way the county's been hounding me. It's absurd; the vines have been there longer than their rules."

"Don't try to make sense of things," Mike smirked. "Napa's a different beast, but not unlike the crazy regulations and Congress hearings we had to endure in the days of Ai-driv3, remember?"

"You can say that again," John sighed.

"Well, my friend, get ready to get your butt kicked," Mike added, playful but deadly serious. "If I can't beat you in the cellar, I'll beat you here."

Fate had other plans. The final throws left no doubt, Boccelaw clinched a fifth consecutive title. The Hotshots fell short again.

As the last points were tallied, John lifted a ball in triumph, then paused. The sky had turned a strange, hazy gray, a faint acrid smell on the breeze. "Shitballs," muttered Kristine, clutching her phone. She and her husband, Tod, John's attorney, owned an iconic vineyard on Howell Mountain they'd dubbed Kristodd. "I hope this isn't on Howell."

"Probably just someone barbecuing…" John tried, though his voice betrayed him.

"No barbecue smells like that," Mike said grimly. "This is another fire. God, I hope it's not a repeat of 2017."

That year, the fires came late, after most of the harvest was in. Now, only a few whites had been picked. Reds still hung heavy. The atmosphere shifted from celebration to dread. One by one, players abandoned the court. Everyone there had ties to the wine business; tight jaws, worried eyes, they hurried to their cars. The match was over. The real fight was about to begin.

Quinzième

"Firefighters To The Rescue"

On August 17, 2020, Paul ducked into Finn's small office at the club. They were huddled over paperwork, discussing what it would take for Paul's young brand, Caitlin, to join Vintner's Collective. Pouring alongside wineries whose wines are made by legends like Andy Erickson, Thomas Brown, Russell Bevan, Helen Keplinger, and his mentor Jacques Rousseau would legitimize his project overnight. But the pandemic had wrecked his otherwise promising launch, he needed help selling.

The day was already surreal. The sky above Napa glowed apocalyptic orange, thick with smoke from the Hennessey fire. Visibility shrank to a few feet; everyone wore N95 masks for smoke and the virus alike. In the courtyard, Kitchen Collective had become a sanctuary for exhausted firefighters.

Tables were laden with hot meals; laughter mingled with fatigue as men and women covered in soot grabbed plates and fueled up.

Inside, Finn was finishing with Paul when a flicker on the screen froze him. His stomach dropped. On the loading dock feed, Marsha, his dear friend and partner, the club's general manager, was being dragged by her hair down the ramp. The attacker, a dishwasher hired a month earlier, fresh out of prison, clutched a large kitchen knife.

Finn shot out of his chair, shoved Paul aside, and sprinted the length of the club. Bursting through the kitchen doors, he shouted, "Follow me, Marsha's in trouble!" Chefs abandoned stations, pans clattering. Finn grabbed a heavy French rolling pin and charged.

But when they reached the ramp, the fight was already underway. The very firefighters they had just fed had hurled themselves into action, swarming the assailant. Shouts filled the air as they wrestled him down. "A couple of quick kicks knocked the knife from his hand, and within seconds the man was pinned."

Marsha stood trembling—hair disheveled, face bruised, eyes wide, but alive. The wildfire's surreal glow pressed in from beyond the courtyard, casting everything in a hellish light.

Paul arrived, chest heaving, and froze. Nothing like this ever happened in the wine business, he thought. Marsha, shaken, was being tended by a calm, steady firefighter. She managed a weak, uneasy smile toward Finn; he returned it with visible relief. Then he turned to Paul, blank face, hollow eyes. In that moment Paul saw it clearly: the look of a defeated man.

He had built Kitchen Collective as a place of joy. Five years on, COVID was draining the life from it. Now, with fire raging outside and violence inside, he knew the dream was finished. This attempted murder on an apocalyptic day was the final blow. The doors would soon close forever.

Seizième

"Buried Secrets"

That spring, Jason Moretti and his crew arrived at dawn with massive vineyard tractors, backhoes, and hydraulic vine pullers. The day had come: Marco Belladono's tangled old family vineyard was about to be torn from the earth. He felt a knot of apprehension, maybe even guilt. What would Nonno say?

The process was methodical: cut irrigation lines, strip trellises and wires, loosen soil around trunks. And then, too quickly, it was time.

Marco watched nearly a century of labor vanish in hours. Vines that had weathered generations were ripped from the ground with violent efficiency. Roots snapped like brittle bones, dust rose in choking clouds, metallic clatter echoed like percussion. To an untrained eye it was chaos; Marco saw precision, a brutal symphony executed with grace.

Jason moved with calm assurance, his crew in rhythm. He'd done this all his life; destruction came with instinctive ease.

At dusk, all that remained were perfectly lined rows of vines and trellises, piled twenty feet wide, ten feet tall, like the aftermath of some ancient harvest. Jason strode toward the shed where Marco stood, holding a few rusted odds and ends. The clamor outside was deafening; inside, the air felt muffled.

With a mischievous grin, Jason hid his hands behind his back. "Took us years to finally clear this damn vineyard. How long's it been since you and I first made this plan, Marco?"

"Too long," Marco said. "I never imagined it would take this long to get financing and start the project. The fires didn't help either. Thank you, brother, for sticking with me, and for wrangling permits and everything else."

"No sweat," Jason said. "And no worries about your grandfather's sangio. I grafted some cuttings onto 110R for you. It's a very vigorous, drought-tolerant rootstock. You've got a short row behind the barn, Marco."

"That's so cool, Jason," Marco said with a grin. "The legacy lives on, thanks to you."

"All good, bud," Jason replied. "And hey, you won't believe what my guys dug up."

Marco smirked. "What—my dad's favorite pruning shears from the '90s?"

"Close, we did find a couple. But… we found something a little more sinister." With a "ta-da," he revealed a torn jacket and a rusted revolver. "Can you even believe this? This gun's been in the ground a long time, but not too long. From the looks of it, I'd say it's a 7-shot Taurus Model 66. If I'm right, they stopped making these around 2010." He grinned. "I only know because my father gave me that same revolver when I turned thirty!"

Marco's chest tightened. The sight jolted a memory, a blurred night back in 2015, too much wine, a couple strong cocktails. Finding the gun. Panicking. Burying it in a shallow grave at the back of the vineyard. Until this moment, he'd forgotten. His stomach turned, but he forced a wide-eyed surprise, pushing down the heat of a blush. "For a second I thought you were about to say you'd found a body," he laughed, almost convincingly. "Still, that's fucking weird."

"Fucking weird is right," Jason said.

"I forgot how much you love guns," Marco deflected. "No one knows them like you. How many are you up to now?"

"Hundreds," Jason smirked. "I've lost count, really." He paused, expression shifting, and lifted the torn jacket again, studying it. He frowned in confusion; then his face lit with astonishment. Using the sleeve, he wiped grime from the revolver's butt and burst into laughter. "Marco, this is my gun! And that's my jacket! What the fuck? My dad gave me this piece years ago. I know it's mine because it's inscribed, look, right there." He spat lightly on the steel and rubbed it clean until letters came clear: JM etched into the base of the grip. "See? My initials."

Marco leaned in, throat tightening. For years he'd thought the weapon belonged to Edward, the neighbor whose feud ended in murder and suicide. He'd panicked, convinced the revolver might somehow tie him to the tragedy, and buried it. Now, staring at those initials, he saw the nonsense of it all. He'd had nothing to do with that crime. He probably should have handed the gun to the sheriff that day. Instead, paranoia had steered him, a secret he carried like a stone.

And the revolver wasn't Edward's. It was Jason's.

Marco forced a smile, stomach lurching. He would have to tell Jason what he had done—how he'd found it, hidden it, misunderstood. The thought of confessing made his throat close. The fallout might be worse than the secret.

So he laughed instead. "Maybe you dropped it from your truck by mistake. You drive like a madman, after all."

"Well, shit," Jason said. "I can't believe this. Dad must've been watching over me today. Guess it's a mystery that'll never be solved, but I'm just glad to have my dad's revolver back!" He turned, striding toward his crew. "¡Vámonos, amigos, está listo! We'll finish tomorrow!" Climbing into his truck, he cranked the engine, waved, and called with a grin, "Bye-bye, farmer boy, see you tomorrow."

Marco waved back, smiling, his chest lighter than it had felt in years. Relief washed over him. The old vineyard was gone, leaving a blank canvas, and with it, the chance for the Belladono legacy to live on.

Jason, as usual, was driving far too fast on the way back. Dust from the vine removal his crew had just finished coated the windshield, reducing visibility to the small patch he'd wiped earlier on the driver's side with a quick swipe of his sleeve. He could hear it all—the dust, the twigs, the pebbles—rattling past and scratching at the truck's paint.

Oh hell, he thought. Another truck getting all fucked up.

He didn't slow down.

He hated the next part: pulling onto Highway 29 from the east side, having to cross both lanes to head south toward Napa. He'd planned to stop by Central Valley to pick up hardware for his next project. A quick glance north, then south. Heavy foot. He went for it.

Out of nowhere, a Volvo appeared on the passenger side.

From that moment on, everything slowed. He saw the blonde woman clearly, her face frozen, eyes locked on him. They reacted at the same instant. She slammed on the brakes, or rather, the Volvo's collision system did it for her, while Jason hit the accelerator and cranked the wheel hard, cutting briefly onto the wrong side of the road.

No cars coming north. They missed each other by inches.

Jesus Christ, he thought. That was close. Where the hell did she come from?

Having almost no visibility through the windshield hadn't helped. He eased onto the shoulder and stopped. As the Volvo passed, he glanced over once more at the young woman. She didn't look back. Her eyes stayed fixed on the road ahead, her speed cautious, almost exaggerated.

Thank God, he thought. She drives like a grandma.

For some inexplicable reason, as he wiped the windshield of his truck, more carefully this time, he found himself thinking of Laura, the woman from the Geezers days whom he had let slip away long ago. It wasn't entirely random; an existential threat has a way of sharpening introspection. What he could not have imagined was that the young woman he had nearly rammed into was Laura's daughter. In a small valley like Napa, six degrees of separation feels far more plausible, where everyone knows everyone.

He told himself that if a moment like the one he had missed back then ever came again, he would have the sense to pursue it and not let it slip away. Unbeknownst to Jason, this would not be the last time their paths crossed.

Seize et demi

"The Phoenix Rising"

Juliet was at work at the Orchard, the old folks' home, when the building suddenly seemed to buzz with chatter. She hurried out of her office, found Liz, one of the nurses, and asked what was going on. Liz explained that the residents were in a frenzy, the word was that something was happening in Bill Weir's room.

Bill, known among the staff as Don Juan, had quite a reputation. Both residents and some of the older staff thought he was handsome, and Juliet could see why. She had met him many times in her office and knew just how disarmingly charming he could be. But as his psychiatrist, she also knew far too much about him to fall under the spell he cast so easily on others.

Juliet strode briskly toward Bill's room, and as she turned the corner, she spotted half a dozen women clustered around his door. The moment they saw her, they scattered like startled birds. A ripple of unease ran through her. Could Bill have had a heart attack?

When she reached the door, she paused, pressing her ear against it out of caution. What she heard made her blink in disbelief: more than one woman giggling, punctuated by Bill's unmistakable grunts.

She banged on the door. "What's going on in there, Mr. Weir? I'm coming in!"

The room erupted in commotion—thuds, clattering objects, muffled shrieks. With no choice left, Juliet pushed the door open.

What she saw could never be unseen. Three bodies, naked and tangled, thrashing on the floor where they had toppled. Bill, trousers bunched around his ankles, was still trying to regain his balance as the two women flailed helplessly, entangled in the chaos.

Juliet gasped. "Mr. Weir, what on earth—!"

The old wrinkly man finally hauled himself upright and, in all his naked splendor, gave a sly bow. "At your service!"

Juliet was mortified. Her face flushed red with embarrassment as she spun around and barked, "Mrs. Winslet, Mrs. Johansson, please get dressed and leave the room at once."

The two women hurried to comply, though as eighty-year-olds their "hurry" felt interminably long. They giggled the whole time, still breathless with mischief, until they finally shuffled off down the hall.

"Oops, Doctor!" Bill called after her. "I didn't realize it was you without my glasses. I thought our appointment wasn't until this afternoon!"

"Mr. Weir, this is unacceptable behavior," Juliet snapped. "We'll be discussing it at four o'clock sharp."

She slammed the door behind her and strode away, her heels clicking hard and fast down the hallway. But once she was well out of sight, the absurdity of the scene caught up with her. Juliet slowed to a stop, covered her mouth, and burst into muffled laughter, shaking her head. By the time she passed the nurses' station she had composed herself again, her stride brisk and professional. She rolled her eyes and smirked. "The kids are at it again," she muttered.

Dix-Septième

"Love At First Chop"

Driving home in her Volvo, Juliet felt safe—she loved the lines of the SUV, which struck her as both solid and classy. She cruised south on Highway 29, NPR humming in the background, when her phone rang. Thank goodness for hands-free, she thought, tapping the console.

While fussing with the screen, she caught movement in the corner of her eye. A huge, dusty white pickup truck burst out of a dirt road on the left side of the highway, appearing out of nowhere. Her car was already chiming, warning that danger was imminent.

She froze.

She looked straight into the face of the scruffy man behind the wheel.

Her Volvo's collision-avoidance system did most of the braking for her. She veered onto the shoulder as the truck overcorrected, drifting briefly into the northbound lane before snapping back in front of her. The driver slowed and pulled over to the side of the road.

For a moment, she wanted to slow down too. She was dying to get a closer look at the crazy man who had almost collided with her, but decided to be extra cautious and keep her eyes on the road instead. All of it happened in a fraction of a second.

Her phone was still ringing.

She took a breath and answered.

Paul's voice filled the cabin, warm and cheerful.
"Hi, lovely Juliet. How was your day?"

"You can't imagine," she said. "A truck almost rammed me off the road. I barely escaped—thank God for the Volvo. The car hit the brakes before I even realized what was happening."

Paul's voice shifted immediately, calmer, steadier.

"I'm so glad we bought that car," he said. "Worth every penny. Are you okay, my love?"

"Yes," Juliet replied, surprising herself with how cheerful she sounded. "I'm past it now. But that's not even the craziest thing that happened today."

There was a pause.

"There's more?" Paul asked.

"I saw things today I can't unsee," she said. "I'll tell you everything when I get home."

"Great… can't wait to hear… my love, let's go to… favorite place for dinn… tonight, I… reservation." His voice crackled, fading in and out.

"Paul, I can't hear you," Juliet said. "I'm hitting the Yountville signal vortex, hold on…"

A garbled murmur came through: "…Did you hear… said…Coles…"

A minute later, she tried again. "Paul, can you hear me now? I'm past Yountville. Did you say you made a reservation at Coles?"

"Oh good, you're back. I hate that dead zone!" Paul replied and continued in franglais. "Oui, I made a reservation pour ce soir à dix-neuf heures. It's Friday, we've got the weekend off, I thought we'd have some fun. Maybe tomorrow we'll even drive out to the coast."

Juliet blinked, surprised by his cheerful tone. Spontaneity wasn't usually Paul's forte, but she welcomed it. And she couldn't wait to share her story from earlier—the outrageous Bill Weir incident—though of course, without names. Patient confidentiality had to be respected… even if the entire facility already knew.

Cole's Chop House was a Napa staple, one of the oldest and most beloved restaurants in town, and Juliet and Paul's favorite haunt. The Oysters Rockefeller and the 21-day dry-aged U.S.D.A. Porterhouse were perennial standouts. That night, the restaurant shimmered with strings of soft lights across the courtyard, casting everything in a golden, magical glow. They loved dressing up for dinner, and tonight was no exception: Juliet wore a long, curve-hugging red dress with sleeves to the wrist, a gown that left Paul unable to take his eyes off her.

They were fortunate to land one of the coveted tables with plush leather banquette seating. They had barely settled in when a cork popped just behind Juliet, making her jump. To her surprise, the champagne was for them.

"A little gift for my favorite regulars," said Eric Keffer, the owner himself, standing there with his trademark smile and easy charm.

"Hi, Eric," they chimed in unison. Paul added, "Thank you so much, that wasn't necessary."

"Speak for yourself," Juliet teased with a mischievous smile.

Eric laughed. "You two are my favorite people, especially Juliet. She's much cuter than you, Paul!"

Paul grinned, his gaze lingering on Juliet. "I totally agree. What's not to adore?"

The exchange made Juliet raise a brow. This was unusual. With a quick, curious scan, she sized up the room. Paul looked a touch nervous, but nothing that stood out. The bartenders and servers bustled as always. Nothing seemed out of place. Relaxing, she began recounting her day. "Then the man stood up, completely nude, blue pills scattered at his feet, and said, 'At your service!'"

Paul burst into laughter, nearly falling off his seat. He had heard plenty of her outrageous nursing-home stories, but this one outdid them all. Juliet laughed with him, then casually glanced back at the menu, only to notice the date printed at the top: July 7, 2021.

She paused for a moment. That was the day they first met, right here at Cole's Chop House, six years ago. Then her eyes fell to the dessert section. It had been replaced with four words: WILL YOU MARRY ME?

She gasped. When she looked up, Paul was already on one knee beside her. "Juliet, I love you more than anything. I don't want to spend another day without you. Please, will you marry me?" He held the wedding ring carefully in both hands. Juliet noticed right away that it wasn't a diamond; Paul knew how much she hated them. Instead, he'd asked a jeweler friend to craft a one-of-a-kind rose gold band, set with a luminous amber-hued sapphire.

Juliet's eyes softened as she took the ring from his hands. "It's beautiful," she whispered. "I love it."

The restaurant hushed, every diner watching, the air buzzing with anticipation. Paul smiled bravely, though his voice carried a tremor. "Say yes soon, my knees are killing me on this floor and everyone's—"

She silenced him with her fingers against his lips. "Oui, bien sûr, Paul. I will marry you."

Still teary-eyed, Juliet carefully slid the ring onto the fourth finger of her left hand. It fit perfectly. "Good job, my love," she said softly. Smiling, she ran her hand through his hair in one quick, affectionate motion. The spotlight above caught it just right, shifting its color from light brown to auburn. She thought it was adorable. She giggled as she deliberately messed his perfect haircut with her right hand, while with the other she admired the sparkle of the sapphire he had chosen for her. Holding it up to the light, she felt at ease and content. Paul was everything she had ever hoped for.

The room erupted in cheers, laughter, and applause. Guests and staff called out congratulations as the energy swelled, then, just as quickly, the restaurant slipped back into its warm hum. Plates clinked, glasses refilled. Their server arrived with the crab salad Paul had pre-ordered, as if nothing extraordinary had happened at all— except that everything had.

Paul exhaled deeply, a quiet relief settling over him. For the first time that night, he allowed himself to simply smile, savor, and enjoy.

Dix-Huitième

"The Private investigator"

Mike had been divorced a couple of years, and he liked the freedom. He was seeing someone, but they both enjoyed their separate lives in their own homes. She was sweet, independent, and perfectly content with the arrangement, so was he.

He lounged in his living room on a modern leather recliner, the kind of piece that, like every-thing else in his house, came from Restoration Hardware. After the divorce, he'd remodeled the entire place in a single day by flipping through the catalog. Cost hadn't mattered; he had more money than he could ever spend. The only corner of the house that stirred real nostalgia for him was his of-fice. It was packed to the hilt with memorabilia.

Every inch of every surface, walls and floors alike, was covered with old cameras and tintypes from his father's collection, diecast cars, cast iron objects of all sorts, books on collecting, Persian rugs, and volumes on the old masters like Rembrandt, Leonardo da Vinci, Caravaggio, and many others. A couple of watercolors his mother had painted hung among them, somewhat clumsy but precious to him nonetheless. She had died when he was in his early teens, and to his lasting regret, she never got to see how successful he would become.

She had always told him, "Micky, you are meant for greatness. I am sure of it." Before saying it, she would briskly rub her palms together to warm them, cup his chubby cheeks, and plant a sweet kiss on his lips. He remembered it vividly. As he grew older, Mike would twist his head away to avoid the ritual, something he later came to regret.

Among the rugs spread across the hardwood floors lay several Navajo pieces he had brought back from a trip to the pueblo, a Turkoman

Tekke from the mid-nineteenth century, and a beautiful Kazak prayer rug with vivid colors of imperial yellow, burnt orange, red, and cinnabar green, covered with strange stick-figure animals throughout. He had spent a great deal on that one at auction, not long after receiving his first large dividend check from AI-Drive3. The rest of the room was blanketed with small Pueblo artworks, Moroccan and Asian artifacts. Some objects hanging on top of a corner bookshelf were gathering dust but brought him great pride, including several pieces of firefighter paraphernalia, among them a fire chief's helmet that had belonged to his grandfather.

This was his temple of creativity, a calm place where he often drifted into memories of childhood. None of these mementos or precious antiques were meant to be shared with guests. It was his private sanctum, a place that grounded him, a place to escape, a place that brought him pure joy.

On the screen, Fox News blared, something he almost never watched. Today, though, he wanted to sample what "the other side" was hearing, what the far right was manufacturing. As expected, it was the same recycled outrage: stolen elections, Fauci conspiracies, mask mandates as hoaxes, and the January 6th attack recast as a "peaceful protest." Antifa was blamed, though Mike admitted he'd never really known what Antifa was supposed to be. Nor did "woke" politics mean anything to him, except during the endless arguments he and John Remington always had at their get-togethers.

He muted the noise, then shut the TV off altogether. Enough nonsense. Turning back to his computer, his eyes fell again on the results that had landed in his inbox just weeks earlier from Ancestry.com.

Two discoveries had stunned him. The first was harmless, even amusing: contrary to what his parents had always insisted, he wasn't British at all. He was mostly Irish and Scottish, with a thread of Acadian French woven in.

But the second discovery was seismic. While browsing potential matches, he had stumbled across one that practically shouted from the screen: 3,468 cM shared DNA. The report was blunt, at that level, it could only mean one thing. A daughter.

The name attached to the match was Juliet M—Mike froze, bewildered. A daughter? Impossible. No woman he had ever been with had claimed she was pregnant, let alone had his child. Then he noticed the profile was "managed by Juliet Moriarty." That surname struck him like a faint echo. Moriarty. He dug back through decades of memory until a face surfaced: Laura Moriarty, a woman he had dated in early-nineties. Could Juliet be her daughter? And had she kept her mother's maiden name?

He had decided to hire a private investigator to help him unravel the mystery. She'd told him over the phone that she already had some news, something that would surely surprise him. Mike had been restless all afternoon, unable to sit still, glancing at the clock every few minutes. The meeting was set for 4:00 p.m.

At 3:59 sharp, the doorbell rang. He strode briskly up the few steps to the entrance and pulled the door open. The person on the threshold didn't hesitate, stepping inside with an air of practiced confidence.

"I'm Roger Harrisson," the investigator said, extending a hand. "It's nice to finally meet you, Mike."

"You don't look like a Brooke Callahan to me," Mike said, his voice edged with suspicion and surprise. Roger towered over Mike. He had long dark-gray hair tied in an odd little bun and a piercing, wolf-like stare from his gray eyes. He was wiry but solidly built. Mike, by contrast, was a bit pudgy from one too many trips to the French Laundry. He was still a good-looking man, just the type you might overlook in a crowd. What he did have going for him was a thick wave of reddish hair, a well-kept, distinguished beard, and bright blue eyes that always seemed to smile with empathy.

Roger gave a small, knowing smile. "Brooke got pulled onto a murder–insurance fraud case at the last minute. She asked me to step in and deliver the results of our search on Juliet Moriarty."

"Mike, we found her. And you were absolutely correct, she may very well be Laura's daughter." Roger tapped the folder he carried, then flipped it open. "Juliet was born on April 16, 1993, in San Bruno, California. She's thirty years old today. That fits perfectly with when you were seeing Laura Moriarty back in '92."

Mike leaned forward, eyes fixed on the papers as Roger turned more pages. "The mother grew up in Napa, but is living in Millbrae now. Widowed five years ago after a sudden illness. She reverted to her maiden name and never remarried. It's all here." He slid the documents across the table, pointing as he spoke.

Then Roger paused, almost savoring the moment. "And now for the pièce de résistance. Juliet Moriarty is alive and well. She's a psychiatrist"—Another pause, sharper this time. "And she lives right here in Napa Valley."

Mike sat back, stunned. He had a daughter. A thirty-year-old woman who could have walked right past him in Napa without either of them knowing.

Roger slid another document from the folder. "We also managed to obtain her phone number, should you want to contact her. And her current address, she used to live in St. Helena, but she's now in Napa's historic downtown."

Mike's throat felt dry, but Roger wasn't finished. "We also located information about the man she's been seeing for the past five years," Roger continued. "A fairly well-known winemaker here in the Valley. It's all in the file—along with much more."

Mike exhaled slowly, trying to steady himself. "I'm still in shock," he admitted. "But deeply grateful for the remarkable work you and your team have done. As promised, here's the check, ten thousand, per our agreement." He gave him the check and shook his hand warmly.

Roger nodded. "Thank you, Mr. Johnson. Don't hesitate to reach out if you have further questions. And remember, if you need us to dig deeper, we'll be ready."

Mike rose, escorting him to the door. "No, I'm sure this will suffice," he said firmly, though his voice betrayed a trace of unease. He opened the door. "Take care, Roger."

The PI gave a courteous nod and stepped out into the fading afternoon light, leaving Mike alone with the folder that might change everything.

Dix-neuvième

"Noble Cheat"

John was immensely proud of his Remington Napa Valley auction lot. This year he was showcasing the crown jewel of his cellar: a single barrel of Martenas Vineyard Cabernet Sauvignon, the finest his team had crafted. The 2021 growing season had been dry, resulting in smaller yields, and though some experts claimed the early September harvest shaved a touch of depth from the fruit, the vintage was still widely regarded as excellent.

It followed a disastrous year. In 2020, fires had torn through Napa and Sonoma just before the red varietals were picked. Entire businesses, wineries, hotels, shops, restaurants had suffered, and smoke taint had marred much of the crop. Unlike 2017, when most fruit was safely harvested before the flames, many estates simply skipped bottling their 2020 wines altogether. John had been among them. He released nothing. Which meant all his hopes, all his pride, were riding on 2021.

And it was magnificent. In John's mind, this Cabernet could stand toe to toe with Scarecrow, the perennial darling of the auction, whose lots had fetched breathtaking sums in years past, at times soaring to a quarter million dollars.

This time, John wasn't leaving anything to chance. He intended to win, whatever the cost. In conversations with fellow vintners, he had learned what many whispered, but few admitted publicly: much of the bidding was quietly fueled by friends of the winery. Call it collusion, call it strategy, it was understood as noble cheating. After all, the proceeds funded wellness programs, health services, and early childhood education across the Valley. Everyone won in the end.

So John devised his own plan. He called in favors from Silicon Valley friends, top buyers, distributors, and retailers. The instructions were simple: drive the price up as high as needed. Outbid everyone, including Scarecrow. And whoever ended up the winner would be reimbursed in full, with the added bonus of exclusive large-format etched bottles, crafted just for them.

The rules of the game were clear.
There were no rules.

The procession of restless tasters eager to sample the new cult wine, Remington, stretched on for hours. John's hand grew weary from wielding the wine thief, filling glass after glass in an endless rhythm. Yet each time someone leaned in and declared his wines the best of the entire auction, a surge of energy shot through him, pushing the fatigue aside. Hundreds of wineries were pouring all around, including his friend Mike, just around the corner, and the buzz of praise was contagious. John felt his pulse quicken; the prelude was over. Now came the real contest, the battle of the paddle.

Everyone gathered around the white boards, each one marked for a particular winery. Organized alphabetically, Remington Estate's board sat right beside Scarecrow's, making the rivalry almost tangible. The numbers on Remington's lot began to climb, inch by inch, as John's friends cautiously raised their paddles, easing themselves into the rhythm of the auction.

Some of John's friends were distracted, still savoring bites from Meadowood, Zuzu, Angele, Charter Oak, and countless other top restaurants with booths around the perimeter. Others were half-drunk, lingering at tables where cult producers poured one masterpiece after another. Where else in the world could you stroll past so many star winemakers in one place? Russell Bevan was drawing crowds with his Tench Vineyard Cabernet Sauvignon, a winery adjacent to the famed Screaming Eagle. No wonder everyone wanted to taste this elixir of the gods. Bevan poured generously—enough to make anyone forget their obligations, or even their own name.

Even Mike had abandoned his own barrel station, drifting among luminaries like Abreu, Carte Blanche, Patel, Schrader, and Promontory. That's when he spotted his towering friend Chris Carpenter, winemaker for Cardinale, impossible to miss at well over six feet tall.

"Chris!" Mike bellowed above the noise. "How's it going? What's the feedback? Can I get a taste?"

He'd already been partaking, helping himself generously from his own barrel, and was a touch more jovial than usual.

Chris dipped the wine thief, pulling a generous pour—more than he'd given anyone else. His deep, gravelly voice carried without effort. "This is a Bordeaux blend from Cardinale, five varietals, with sixty-five percent Cab sourced from Mount Veeder. Tell me what you think Mike. Feedback's been strong, and the scoreboard's looking good. We're sitting at twelve thousand for a case—not bad, eh?"

Mike swirled, sipped, and grinned. "It's fantastic, Chris... oh, hell!" In a flash he remembered his real task: bidding for John. He bolted toward the Remington board, arm shooting up with his paddle before he'd even stopped running.

Through the roar of the crowd he heard the amplified voice: "Sold!"

A young woman appeared in front of him, clipboard in hand, asking for his name and paddle number. He caught the glint of her name tag and froze.

Juliet. Juliet Moriarty.

The odds rattled him. His chest tightened.

"My name—uh—Mike. Mike Johnson. Paddle number..." He glanced down and read it aloud. "Nine-one-one."

Fitting, he thought grimly, because all he wanted to do was run. Instead, he steadied himself, thankful for the wine, just enough to take the edge off. He drew a breath and asked,

"Is your mom… Laura Moriarty?"

Juliet blinked, stunned for a beat, then her face lit up. In a room full of wealthy strangers, someone actually knew her mother. "Yes! How did you guess? Do I know you? How do you know my mother?"

But the roar of bidding swelled around them, drowning their words. Juliet was called back to her task, jotting down the names of winners, lucky or otherwise. Lucky when they meant to buy. Unfortunate when they hadn't realized that every case marked beside their name was now contractually theirs, no matter the steep price tag, their reputation was on the line.

Mike, his voice carrying a trace of emotion, asked quietly, "Juliet, could I have your business card? I'd like to reach out next week and talk. I have a winery in Oak Knoll, maybe we could meet there?"

Juliet didn't hesitate. "Of course, Mike. Here's my card. I'm a psychiatrist at the Orchard Senior Living Community, not to be confused with the awesome hotel in Carneros," she said with a smile. "My husband's a winemaker, and that's why I love volunteering at the Auction."

All around them, the room swelled with cheers, applause, and the thunder of victory, bidders shouting, auctioneers booming "Sold!" until the air vibrated with celebration.

Mike raised his voice once more. "I'll call you!"

Juliet shot him a quick thumbs-up before vanishing back into the crowd, gone as swiftly as she had appeared.

By the time Mike found his friend John, the celebration was already in full swing. Remington had taken the top spot at the auction, and the victory was going to cost John a fortune, but he couldn't have cared less. He had crushed all his competitors, and by a wide margin. This win didn't just cement his cult status, which he already commanded; it placed Remington Estate shoulder to shoulder with Napa's most legendary names: Screaming Eagle, Harlan and Tusk.

Mike longed to share the extraordinary moment he had just experienced, possibly meeting his daughter for the very first time. But he knew this wasn't the moment. Instead, he wrapped his friend in a firm embrace and congratulated him on the big win.

Vingtième

"Checkmate"

Marco was playing chess at Napa Valley Coffee Roasting Company, his favorite spot in St. Helena. Every Thursday morning, he met Floyd Matthis there for a game. Floyd was the new Director of Winemaking at Nine Stones, where the iconic Hood Vineyard sprawled in all its splendor atop Pritchard Hill. He was also spearheading an exciting project, Bluemont Cabernet from the famed Las Posadas Vineyard, something so extraordinary Marco dreamed of emulating in his own wines. Maybe his friend would help him reach that goal.

"Checkmate," Floyd said with a grin. "Looks like I got the best of you this time." He hadn't even finished when he felt a friendly tap on his shoulder. Floyd looked up, and there stood Jacques Rousseau, his old mentor, smiling as he said hello.

"I always know where to find you, Floyd," Jacques teased. "I guess it takes a lot of good coffee to make great wine!"

"Hi, Jacques," Floyd laughed. "Yes, it sure does, and your presence here proves that point."

Floyd turned to him, "Hey Jacques, meet my friend Marco. He just finished planting a Cab vineyard in Yountville. He sucks at chess, but the guy can farm!"

"Good to meet you, Marco," Jacques said warmly. "Where's that vineyard of yours?"

Marco froze for a moment—this was Jacques Rousseau in the flesh, the man behind so many of Napa's greatest wine projects over the last few decades. He gathered himself and stammered out in a nervous, almost skittish tone, "Good to meet you, Jacques… I've heard so many great things about you, I can't believe I'm actually meeting you… It's such an honor…"

Suddenly, Marco felt a sharp kick under the table. He glanced at Floyd, who arched his brows and gave him the look—the universal stop rambling before you make a fool of yourself warning.

Marco: "Well, like I was saying, good to meet you, Jacques." He cleared his throat. "My vineyard is right across the highway from the restaurant Brix. To finance this, I sold a parcel of property which the developer named after my family, The Belladono Hotel," he added proudly.

Jacques: "It's a beautiful hotel Marco, you must be proud" — "I heard of this project from my friend Jason Moretti. Sounds like you've got some good soil there, great potential I've heard."

Marco gleamed with pride. He couldn't believe his ears, Jacques Rousseau had heard of his project. "Thank you, Jacques. My friend Jason and

I just finished planting it with Clone 4 and 7. I can't wait to see the results in a couple of years."

Jacques: "If Jason was involved, then I'm sure it will be very special."

Marco, unable to contain his excitement, cut in: "Feel free to check it out one of these days, if you have some free time. Although I guess free time isn't exactly one of those commodities you have much of, is it?"

He glanced at Floyd, who was again giving him the look.

Marco, flustered, added quickly: "Well, Jacques, I won't take more of your time."

Jacques, with a gentle smile, replied: "Absolutely. Maybe Jason and I will stop by one of these days. You never know, I might need high-quality fruit for the plethora of projects I'm working on!" — "Will you be making any wines from your vineyard, Marco?"

Without missing a beat, Marco replied, "I ran out of money planting that vineyard. So the dream of building a winery is on hold for now. But I'll surely make a little Cabernet under my Belladono label. I have to keep that legacy going, maybe my kids will build that winery one day!"

"You never know," Jacques said, nodding.

Then, turning to Floyd, he added, "I'll be seeing you up on Pritchard Hill soon, unless, of course, they end up selling it to Rehm Cellars." Both men knew the possibility of that deal was very real.

"That would be a sad day," Floyd admitted. "I love working with Hood Vineyard Cab."

Jacques leaned in. "By the way, Floyd, can you do me a favor? See if David Abreu up at Las Posadas might have any fruit available. I'd love to get my hands on some for a few projects I'm working on. I love the Cabernet and Cab Franc that come from there. I'm looking for something dark, complex, cassis, opulent, with that earthy dried herb character. A bit like your Bluemont cab." His smile turned mischievous.

"Unless I grab it first," Floyd teased. "Who knows? Maybe I'll get a hundred points from Parker and go from seventy-five cases to a thousand. I might let you have a ton or two," he said bursting into laughter.

"I'll take whatever I can get," Jacques replied, with a smile.

"Alright, I've got to get going, guys." Jacques shook hands with Marco and Floyd, then started toward the door. He barely made it five feet before someone intercepted him with a bear hug and launched into a fresh conversation. From the way Jacques's eyes flicked toward the exit, it was obvious he had no time, or bandwidth, for it.

Marco asked Floyd, "Do you think he means it? He might actually come by and check my vineyard?" — "Jacques is a man of his word," Floyd said. "Don't worry—I'll remind him. Once you're ready and have some wines from that vineyard, we can have him taste them."

"I've got to go, Marco. See you next Thursday."

"You got it. see you then!" Marco replied.

"A Mother's Confession"

A couple of weeks later, Mike welcomed Juliet and Paul for a small gathering at his winery. The thought of telling her he might be her father was nerve-racking, to say the least, but he felt it was the right thing to do. Early that morning, Mike had his staff clean everything top to bottom. He also asked Kyle, his vineyard manager, to return all the equipment—the ATVs and tractor—neatly to the barn, and to do an early thinning in the vineyard, dropping excess fruit where clusters were crowding. Mike gave the instructions in an assertive yet nervous tone.

Kyle replied, "I'm on it," though he couldn't help wondering why his boss was being so particular. Why was he suddenly clearing away the empties from a collection of impressive cult wines he'd shared with friends the week before, and why did it all feel so urgent?

Still, Kyle got to work. Six hours later, the vineyard looked pristine. The dropped fruit, however, was to be left scattered on the ground, another strange request, Kyle thought.

Mike knew that Juliet's fiancé was coming, and Paul was none other than the Director of Winemaking for Jacques Rousseau. This guy was a superstar in the wine world, and Mike wanted the vineyard to look the part for his visit. The dropped fruit was a way of showcasing the quality of his viticultural style and philosophy. They usually dropped as much as thirty percent of the fruit before harvest, clusters evenly distributed, combined with mostly dry farming, meticulous canopy management, created more power, depth and concentration in the wines being produced.

Oddly enough, as they drove, "Papa Was a Rolling Stone" by the Temptations floated from the radio. Juliet and Paul exchanged a look, both aware of the irony, and spoke quietly about how best to make the coming conversation as unawkward as possible.

Juliet had already told her mother about the strange encounter with Mike Johnson at the auction. At first, Laura had denied everything: "I have no idea who that man is." But when Juliet pressed harder during a visit to Millbrae, face to face in her mother's kitchen, the truth finally broke through.

"Yes," Laura admitted, tears welling. "Mike was a man I dated briefly in the nineties. We cared deeply for each other, but my career pulled me to the East Coast. Only after I left did I realize I was pregnant. I thought it wasn't fair to derail his future—or mine. So I kept it a secret, and never told a soul… except your late father."

Laura paused, voice trembling. "Not long after, I met him. We fell in love so quickly and married within months. He didn't care that I was carrying another man's child. He raised you, Juliet, and that's all that should matter. He was your father in every way."

Juliet inhaled slowly, then responded in the steady, clear cadence of a psychiatrist—calm, pragmatic, but gentle. "If you felt that was the right decision, then I support you, Mom. At the same time, it might have helped to know sooner, especially after Dad passed. It would have given me space to process this in my own way."

Laura's eyes filled. "I tried… a couple years ago, I almost told you. But I was terrified you'd see me differently."

Juliet reached across the table and took her mother's hand. "Mom, nothing you could say would make me stop loving you. But… I wish you'd trusted me enough to share this burden with me sooner. Finding out from a stranger, at an auction, of all places—" Her voice caught, the clinical evenness slipping. "It felt like the ground shifted under me."

Laura squeezed her hand tightly. "I know, sweetheart. And I regret it every day. I thought I was protecting you—from confusion, from pain, even from Mike. But maybe I was just protecting myself."

Juliet blinked back tears, her professional calm gone. "You should have given me the chance, Mom. I could have handled it. I deserved to know."

"I know," Laura whispered. "And I'm so sorry."

For a long moment, the two women sat in silence, only the hum of the refrigerator filling the space between them. Then Juliet took a steadying breath and softened. "What matters now is the future. Mike exists. He's part of me. I need to know what role—if any—he'll play in my life."

Laura nodded, her expression a mixture of fear and hope. "Then I'll support whatever choice you make. Just promise me one thing, don't let this change how you see the father who raised you. He adored you, Juliet. You were his whole world."

Juliet's face crumpled, tears finally spilling over. "I know. And nothing will ever change that."

Laura pulled her into an embrace. "Then that's enough. We'll face the rest together."

The car turned left onto Oak Knoll Avenue, just off Solano. Paul glanced at Juliet, his voice steady and reassuring. "Don't worry, my love, I've got your back. This will be fine. Finding a father you never knew, right here in Napa Valley… it's nothing short of miraculous, isn't it?"

Juliet exhaled, her eyes fixed on the vineyards rushing past the window. "I still can't believe it, Paul. I'm excited and overwhelmed, all in the same breath."

Paul reached across the console, lacing his fingers through hers. He squeezed firmly, his gaze never leaving the road. "I've got you," he repeated softly.

They pulled up to the gate. With a low hum, the massive wrought-iron doors swung open as if by magic. Juliet leaned forward, reading the inscription arched across the ironwork. The words shimmered in bronze: The Gentleman Farmer.

"That's a cool name for a winery," she murmured.

The driveway stretched on endlessly, flanked by hundreds of silver-leaved olive trees, their branches catching the afternoon light. Beyond them, vineyards unfurled in perfect rows on either side, impeccably manicured, every line straight, every trellis gleaming.

Rounding a final bend, both Paul and Juliet drew in a breath. Before them stood a grand Victorian house, its wide porches and wraparound decks rising like a vision, elegant and imposing, yet warmly inviting.

Mike stood on the porch waving as Paul eased the car beneath a massive oak that looked like it had guarded the land for two hundred years.

"Here goes nothing," Juliet whispered, pulling the door handle. She stepped out, waiting for Paul to join her. She preferred he take the lead; somehow his presence steadied her nerves.

Paul strode toward Mike, extended a firm handshake, and said, "Hi, I'm Paul, Juliet's fiancé. And if I may say so, your vineyards are a sight to behold. Clearly, someone here knows exactly what they're doing."

He glanced aside and noticed Kyle, coiling a hose by the stairs just a few feet away. Kyle looked up with a proud grin, and Paul immediately recognized the quiet force behind the vineyard's perfection.

"Thank you," Mike replied, his tone touched with sincerity. "Coming from you, that's a great compliment."

Juliet finally stepped forward, her nerves tightening as she pushed past Paul. She clasped Mike's hand, looked into his eyes, and froze for a heartbeat, maybe longer. Her breath caught as a thought pulsed through her mind: I can't believe this man is my father. She let go quickly, murmuring, "Your house is lovely, Mike."

"Well, let's head inside," Mike said, his voice carrying a faint hesitation. "I've set up a little wine tasting, and a charcuterie board to boot."

They crossed into the living room, where an imposing staircase curved upward on either side, framing the grand space. Paul and Juliet looked around in awe while Mike, trailing behind, felt his chest tighten. Panic fluttered in his stomach. How am I going to approach this? he wondered. Maybe I should just come straight out with it.

They took a seat on two separate plush, modern settees. The table between them had a glass top resting on what looked to be an old, gnarled vine stand. The charcuterie and cheese tray was magnificent, far more than anyone could eat in one sitting. The bottle of wine on the table was beautifully designed, and the glasses were what Paul immediately recognized as Gabriel, the same ones used at the Rousseau winery. Elegant and versatile across all varietals, but especially Pinot Noir, their design was as functional as it was beautiful.

A long silence ensued, everyone staring at the table—not at its beautiful spread, but because no one quite knew how to begin the dreaded conversation. Finally, Juliet, ever the professional, broke it. She blurted out, almost too quickly, "You can feel at ease, Mike. I've already spoken with my mom, and she told me everything."

Mike leaned forward cautiously. "Oh yes? And… what did she say?"

Juliet took a steady breath and began recounting the story exactly as her mother had told it. Fifteen minutes passed as she spoke, her voice calm and measured.

"And then my mom met my dad—well, the dad who raised me. He was wonderful. He took care of me my whole childhood, but tragically, he passed away from cancer five years ago. He knew the truth and loved me as his own."

At that, Mike gently raised his hand to stop her. Relief washed over his face.

"First of all, I'm very sorry about your dad," he said softly. "And… I'm so glad your mom told you. I can't tell you how relieved I am, and how excited I am to finally get to know you and Paul in a real, meaningful way."

He hesitated, then added: "I only found out myself a couple of months ago, when the DNA results came back from Ancestry. After that, I hired a PI, and he quickly tracked down both you and your mom for me. Thank goodness you'd done your own test with the same company and used your mother's maiden name. Otherwise, we might never have found each other."

It grew emotional for a while, but soon after the warmth settled in, and the rest of the evening flowed so naturally that they felt as if they had never been apart. At the end of the evening, as they were leaving, Mike turned to Paul. He asked if he and Juliet might come back in the next few weeks to walk the property, explore the vineyard, and perhaps tour the winemaking facility.

"I have a proposal," Mike added. "Let's hold off until your next visit—there's a lot more I want to show you first…"

Vingt-deuxième

"The Wedding Plan"

After Mike discovered Juliet was his daughter, he needed time to adjust. Like everyone else, he'd heard of unsolved murders being cracked by DNA, but never in a million years had he imagined finding a child that way. He had never planned on having children, yet now, blessed with a daughter, he was thrilled. Juliet was brilliant, independent, and full of life, surely cut from the same cloth as himself.

She was in love with Paul, a wonderful young man, and was planning to marry him. Mike resolved that neither of them would ever want for anything. His first step would be asking his friend John if they could host the wedding at his estate; Mike's own place was too small, and the county's restrictions, and nosy neighbors, made an "unpermitted" gathering impossible. He wanted to surprise Juliet with a beautiful wedding, fully paid for—a gift from her newly found father. It was his way of making up for the years he had missed, the years he hadn't been there to watch her grow and blossom into the remarkable woman she had become. He had already heard Juliet's version of events, but the real reason her mother had never told him she was pregnant remained a mystery. Perhaps Laura would reveal that secret the next time they met. But that no longer mattered to Mike; his heart was set on nurturing the bond with his daughter and reclaiming some of the lost years.

What mattered now was the future. Juliet would remain in medicine, her true passion, while Paul, after more than a decade of training under the Rousseau family, had emerged as one of Napa Valley's rising stars. If Paul accepted, Mike would invite him to run the winery with full creative freedom. And in time, both he and Juliet would inherit it, securing their future and tying their lives to his forever.

Mike leaned back in his chair, phone pressed to his ear. "Hello, John, it's Mike. Miss me yet?" He let the question hang, then added with a chuckle, "So, you need my help getting your winery to the next level?"

It was pure teasing. Mike's own winery had built a solid reputation in Napa, but it couldn't compare to John's monument on Pritchard Hill. John had gone all out, hiring world-renowned architect Frank Gehry, designer of the Guggenheim Bilbao, to craft an estate as spectacular as the site itself. Pritchard Hill was widely regarded as the crown jewel of American viticulture, rivaling the best terroirs anywhere in the world.

"Ha! What up, dipshit!" John shot back, then laughed. "Just kidding. Yeah, I missed my bud, but no, I don't need help from the likes of you." His laugh was short, clipped; Mike could tell from his tone that John was busy.

Then John shifted back to teasing. "You still have Mr. Nobody making your wine?"

He could afford the jab. After all, John had secured the country's top winemaker, Jacques Rousseau, to oversee his project. With Rousseau at the helm, Remington Estate had become a sensation—success and 100-point scores raining down year after year. In just a few seasons, John's winery had achieved cult status in the Valley.

"Well, actually," Mike said, "I'm thinking of hiring Rousseau's second-in-command to make our wines. He doesn't know it yet, so keep that to yourself, John."

"My lips are sealed."

"Good. Because I actually wanted to ask you a huge favor, I'd like to help plan and fund their wedding. Maybe we could even do it at your place, if you're okay with that?"

"I had no idea they were getting married," John said. "They're perfect for each other." He paused, then added with a playful tone, "How is it you just find out you have a daughter, and then, not long after, you're already planning her wedding? A true model of efficiency!"

"I know, it's astonishing," Mike admitted. "I'm still in shock, but having a daughter, my friend, fills my heart with happiness."

"Okay, okay—you're breaking my heart," John teased. "Guess I've got no choice but to say yes to the wedding at my place. But only if you stop with the tiny violin routine. You know I try not to host too many weddings here, I don't need to give my neighbors a reason to snitch to the county!"

Mike felt a weight lift from his shoulders. "You're the man, John. I mean it—I owe you big time." John laughed. "Damn right you do. And we can't have them getting married in that little shack of yours."

Unfortunately for both men, the county would ultimately get involved in ways neither could have ever expected.

Vingt-troisième

"Harvest of Dreams"

They arrived with Juliet's new dad, Mike, who had invited them for dinner—though Paul suspected the real purpose was to talk about the job offer: General Manager and Winemaker at his estate.

Walking up to the French Laundry together, Paul and Juliet stopped in front of the little stone and brick cottage and looked at each other. "This is it?" Juliet whispered. It looked more like someone's old farmhouse than one of the best restaurants in the world. Ivy climbed the walls, the blue door was simple, and the garden out front smelled faintly of lavender. Across the road, neat rows of vegetables stretched out, as if the place grew its own pantry.

Inside, everything shifted. White linens, fresh flowers, a quiet hum in the room—nothing flashy, just calm and perfect. "It feels like church," Paul murmured, and Juliet squeezed his hand.

When they got a peek into the kitchen, they stared in awe. It looked more like a lab than a kitchen, the stainless steel gleamed, pristine copper pans hanging above the stove, chefs in whites moved in total sync, and the focus was absolute. Above it all, on the wall, hung the words Sense of Urgency. Juliet leaned in and whispered, "Now I get it. This is where magic happens."

They were not seated for long when the maître d', Stewart, approached the table.

"Hi Mike, it's good to see you again. How long has it been?"

"Oh yes, just last week and the week before. Thank goodness for clients like you; you're helping me keep my job secured!" Mike grinned.

He noticed Chef Thomas Keller, wearing his usual crisp whites, step into the dining room, scanning the room with quiet focus.

"It's nice to see Chef Keller always keeping a close eye on the dining room," Mike said.

"Of course," Stewart replied without looking back. "Chef is here almost every day. Nothing escapes him."

"Has he acquired the rest of Yountville yet?" Mike teased with a smile.

The maître d' stayed stoic, pretending not to hear, a self-preservation move Mike suspected.

"What's the medal Chef Keller is wearing around his neck?" Mike asked.

"Oh, that," Stewart said. "A French delegation of master chefs came today and bestowed upon him the title of Maître Cuisinier de France, Master Chef of France. He's the first American to receive it, and he's wearing it proudly today."

"And he should be," Mike exclaimed.

The medal glinted against Keller's whites, a small circle of polished metal that carried the weight of centuries. In that instant, the man who had once stood outside the gates of French kitchens as an outsider had been welcomed inside. The world of haute cuisine had bent ever so slightly, just enough to let in a Napa Valley legend.

Just as chefs Jacky Fréon and Georges Blanc had once been honored, it would be no surprise if the French someday bestowed upon Keller the honorary title of Meilleur Ouvrier de France, the finest craftsman of France. By tradition, the same distinction is even conferred upon the President of the French Republic.

Mike gestured toward his guests. "Please, Stewart, meet my daughter Juliet and her fiancé, Paul Monier."

"Very nice to meet you both," Stewart said warmly. "I believe I know Paul through the Rousseau Atelier."

"Yes," Paul replied a little awkwardly. "I'm their director of winemaking."

"Well, good to finally meet you in person."

Just then, a waiter leaned in to whisper something in Stewart's ear. The maître d' nodded, then excused himself. "Enjoy your dinner," he said, slipping away toward a nearby table.

Mike's gaze followed Chef Keller, who had moved across the room to greet another guest. Mike recognized him immediately, the man he had voted for and hoped would one day be president: the state's governor, a former vintner turned politician. A regular at the French Laundry, like so many other celebrities.

They must have been on their tenth dish by now, not counting the salmon tartare cornet that had greeted them at the start. The next course arrived: herb-roasted, crispy-skinned duck breast laid over a bed of foraged mushrooms.

In that moment, Mike gathered his thoughts and turned to Paul.

"What are your ambitions for the future?" he asked. "Do you plan to work for Jacques Rousseau much longer?"

Paul set down his glass and answered thoughtfully.

"I've been making a little wine over at my buddy Julien's place in Napa. Unfortunately, your friend John has purchased the Martenas Vineyard, and now I've lost my fruit. It's tough to find grapes with that level of quality and name recognition, and even tougher trying to compete with trillionaires. No of-fense to your friend — the game's slightly skewed, isn't it?"

Mike listened intently and nodded.

"I was hoping to slowly grow production and maybe, one day, have my own vineyard," Paul continued. "It might sound crazy, a long shot even, but I'd love to have my own winery one day."

Mike, his voice brimming with excitement, said:

"What if you came to work with me—became my partner, took over as managing partner, and created the wines you've always dreamed of? You could replant with the varietals you believe best suit our terroir, and while waiting for the vineyard to mature, source any fruit you need. And in time, I'll step back, leaving both you and Juliet to carry on the legacy. It's a lot to think about, so I'll let you both talk it over and get back to me whenever you wish."

Paul hesitated before replying. "I don't know, Mike… I don't see how I could come up with the cash to buy in. Your property is much larger than what Juliet and I had in mind."

Mike shook his head, smiling reassuringly. "You don't need to worry about that. I'm happy to give you a ten percent stake and a very comfortable salary. You're family now, I want to give you both a leg up. And let's not forget, Paul, your talent and reputation will help take this winery to the next level."

Juliet interjected, half-laughing, half-protesting.
"Mike, that's too much. We can't let you give away the farm—literally! Paul and I both make good money, and we're doing just fine. Surely we can pay our way forward."

Mike's tone softened, though his conviction remained firm.
"I have more money than I'll ever spend on my own, and I have no children. Please, let me do this. It makes me happy to know I can help you two achieve your dream."

"Speaking of dreams," Mike said, his voice carrying the promise of something even more exciting. "Paul, I think you might forgive John for taking your fruit source after you hear this. I spoke with him about his Remington Estate. As you know, we've been best friends since our college days, and he's offered to let you two use his incredible property for your big day, if you'd like."

Juliet, shocked at first, suddenly burst with excitement. "I love that place! That's incredible—Paul, that place is crazy!"

Paul looked from Mike to Juliet, his face lit with surprise. He let out a long, happy sigh. "Wow… I don't know what to say."

"Just say yes, and I'll take care of everything," Mike replied with a grin. "It's my wedding gift to you both."

Juliet and Paul turned to each other, eyes wide, mouths open in disbelief, then they both burst into laughter and threw their arms around Mike.

Suddenly, the once-quiet dining room filled with a ripple of joy. Guests nearby looked over and smiled knowingly, as if they too could feel that something wonderful had just happened at that table.

Vingt quatrième

"A Love That Burns Bright"

Paul and Juliet arrived early that morning. The valley was in its second flowering, that magical moment when vines are shifting from green to golden to shades of amber and red. Juliet found it mesmerizing. Both were thinking it might be the most important day of their lives. They were focused, giggly, and nervous all at once. It was only their second visit to the winery. Walking up to it, they felt both dwarfed and exhilarated, as though they'd stepped into a piece of art before even entering.

The feeling reminded them of a quick trip they'd taken the year before to San Sebastián and Bilbao, two dazzling towns in Spain's Basque Country. In Bilbao stood one of the world's great architectural masterpieces: the Guggenheim Museum, its sweeping titanium curves wavy and luminous, gleaming and twisting, sprawling into shapes that caught the light differently with every step they took. Juliet's favorite, though, had been Koons' massive flower-covered Puppy at the entrance, a whimsical guardian that had become the Guggenheim's unofficial trademark, as instantly recognizable as the building itself. It was no surprise it reminded them of that structure; after all, Remington Estate had been designed by the same architect.

As soon as they stepped through the towering glass-and-titanium doors, they saw Melissa waiting for them inside. She was Juliet's Maid of Honor, and also Finn's wife. Juliet and Melissa were two peas in a pod: both avid gardeners, and Melissa a self-taught herbalist.

On weekends, it wasn't unusual to find them on day trips to Sebastopol or Forestville, gathering plants, herbs, and flowers—anything they didn't grow themselves or couldn't grow enough of. Damask rose petals for making rose hydrosols. Calendula, comfrey, yarrow for antiseptic salves. And whatever else they could get their hands on.

They had even decided to stop drinking at the same time, supporting each other through the change. Melissa, always organized and unfailingly generous, was a selfless helper. A true friend.

"Hi, you two," greeted Melissa, her face lighting up. "This place is truly unreal—I can't believe you're getting married here today!" Melissa smiled. "I'll tell you something you might not know, a little trivia of sorts," she said. "The architect Frank Gehry once explained in an NPR interview—I want to say it was with Terry Gross—in the early 2000s, that he chose titanium over stainless steel because stainless looks dull on gray days. Titanium, he said, still shines, even turning golden in winter. Interesting, right?"

"Uh!" Juliet muttered, distracted.

"Well anyway, let's get to it. We have lots to do, you two, but first, have you both eaten? Are you hydrated? And have I told you how beautiful and handsome you look? Honestly, you're perfect for each other," Melissa said with a sweet smile.

Paul answered, "Yes, we had a light breakfast at Auberge du Soleil. At sunrise on the deck. It was fabulous."

"Yes, it was so beautiful," Juliet added softly.

Melissa laughed. "I'm jealous. But remember, it's your day. Just a reminder: once we're back later, you won't be seeing each other again until you're at the altar. You in your tux, Juliet in your beautiful wedding dress." She pointed toward the floral archway in the distance.

The altar was already draped in blossoms, white Damask roses with shades of blush and pink. Even from afar, they released a fragrance both complex and delicate, their perfume floating in the air like something magical and timeless. Melissa and Juliet, herbalists at heart, recognized the scent instantly; it was as familiar as it was enchanting.

Melissa went over the timeline: a quick reminder not to forget the rings, the do's and don'ts at the altar, the all-important "I do" and the kiss. She walked them through each step with ease—the Argentinian barbecue dinner to be served outside on the lawn, the cake cutting. "The cake will arrive a little later," Melissa explained. Mike had secured the famous pastry chef Anna Umar, who was coming in person. She and her staff would bring the masterpiece in three separate sections, assemble it on site, and finish it with the floral arrangement Juliet and Melissa had designed together. And then, the final dance.

Juliet had chosen to share that dance with her newly found father, Mike, while Paul would dance with her mother, Laura. Sadly, Paul's own parents couldn't be there, since his father was very ill, and his mother had stayed behind to care for him.

At the end, Melissa looked intently at both of them and said, "We're not aiming for perfect—we're aiming for joyful."

Paul and Juliet replied in unison, "Well said, Melissa!"

Later that afternoon, the cello playing softly, as Paul stood at the altar, his hands clasped tightly in front of him. He was nervous, tried to steady, but sweat ran down his face, this is forever he thought! The air was filled with the delicate perfume of roses, and the low murmur of the guests rising to their feet.

Down the aisle came the children first, two flower girls and a little ring bearer. The girls giggled as they tossed handfuls of pale petals into the air, scattering them like soft confetti across the white runner. One boy, tasked with the pillow and the rings, veered off course and had to be gently steered back down the aisle, his antics drawing soft laughter from the guests.

Behind them, the bridesmaids walked gracefully in step. Melissa, Maid of Honor, radiant in her gown, gave Juliet who was hiding in the corridor, a quick wink as she passed. Tina Carpenter followed, her composure elegant, and then Liz the nurse that she befriended from work, whose warm smile glowed as she reached the altar. On Paul's side, Julien was goofing around and joking with Jacques Rousseau beside him, and last, Paul's disheveled cousin from Dijon, hair still messy from the long flight, his tie slightly askew but his grin impossible to miss.

Then the music shifted. Every head turned.

Juliet appeared at the end of the aisle, radiant in her wedding gown, the silk catching the light like liquid pearl. Her arm was linked with Mike's. The newly found father carried himself with a mix of pride and awe, joyful but emotional as he walked his daughter forward. Juliet held her white bouquet close, her steps measured, graceful, her gaze locked on Paul. Paul's knees nearly gave way at the sight. He thought, this is it — I wish my parents were here, they would love her.

Guests whispered, snapped photos, and held back tears. In one row near the middle, Jason Moretti leaned toward Laura, Juliet's mother, his voice low and warm.

"Hard to believe, isn't it?" Jason said. "I still remember those nights at Geezers, downtown Napa. You in that corner booth with friends, the jukebox blaring. Feels like a lifetime ago."

Laura let out a soft laugh, nostalgia flickering in her eyes. "Geezers. Oh God, I haven't thought about that place in years. Sticky floors, the cool bar top, I think they were beer capsules under that epoxy finish, huge pitchers of beer hanging from the rafters, and everyone thinking they could sing after midnight."

Jason chuckled. "Yeah, and me, pretending not to stare too long whenever you walked in. I had the biggest crush back then, probably obvious, though I thought I was subtle."

Laura tilted her head, amused. "You never said a word."

"Didn't have the guts," Jason admitted, eyes still on Juliet and Mike moving steadily down the aisle. "Life takes you different places. But seeing you now, reminded me, I might have had a crush on you too. Feels like things have come full circle."

Laura's smile softened. "Well, you chose grapes over girls, Jason. And look where that got you."

Jason grinned. "True. Though if I'm being honest, some part of me wonders what might've happened if I'd been braver."

Laura glanced at him, eyes kind but firm. "You were exactly who you needed to be. And I was too. You know Jason, nothing stops you from asking me out now, unless you are seeing someone."

Jason replied quickly and nervously, "Would you go out with me next week, Laura?"

Laura peered into his big, hopeful brown eyes and at that chiseled face with the cute dimples she'd found attractive even back in their twenties. With the most sensual smile Jason had ever seen, she said, "Since Geezers is gone, where are we going?"

To Jason's disappointment, the conversation was interrupted by a sudden hush as Juliet and Mike reached the altar. Mike lingered for a moment, the reality still unfamiliar, Juliet was the daughter he had only come to know a few months ago. With a little hesitation, he gave her a peck on the cheek, placed her hand in Paul's, and stepped aside. The ceremony was underway.

Soon after, the bride and groom exchanged vows meant to last a lifetime. Jason leaned back toward Laura and whispered with a mischievous grin, half joking, "Should we fucking tag along and just get married, the priest is still here?"

Laura and Jason burst out laughing, so hard that the people around them glanced over. And in that instant, they both knew—this, too, was forever.

The courtyard glowed with strings of lights strung between old olive trees, the air alive with laughter and the mouthwatering scent of wood smoke. Everything was going according to Melissa's plan. The only drawback was the wind blowing a little hard, hats and napkins were flying around. A touch annoying, but no more.

A massive parrilla had been fired since dawn, glowing embers sending sparks skyward as the grill master turned racks of ribs with long iron tongs. Whole butterflied lambs, cordero a la cruz leaned against iron crosses over smoldering coals, their fat sizzling in a steady rhythm, perfuming the evening with something primal and irresistible.

Juliet and Paul's guests clustered around high tables with glasses of Malbec in hand, marveling at the spread. Alongside the meats, wooden boards overflowed with empanadas, chorizo and morcilla, grilled provoleta bubbling with herbs, and bowls of chimichurri so green it looked alive.

Jacques and his beautiful wife, Cara, were in deep conversation with John. He was prying gently, curious about how business was going at the Rousseau winery.

"We've had a dip in our visitors and appointments lately," John said. "I'm just wondering, where are you at, Cara?"

With a smile, Cara replied, "We're noticing it too, John. Thankfully, my GM Sylvie is still kicking some butt. Honestly, I'm not sure where we'd be without her."

"True," John said, nodding. "Great employees make or break you."

To which Jacques replied with a smile, "Where would I be without you, my love?" He followed it with a sweet kiss on Cara's cheek.

Cara smiled back and said, "And don't you forget that honey."

John stood up, laughing as he walked away. "I've got to grab a bottle from my cellar—you'll be impressed, Jacques!"

The main feast came in waves: juicy asado de tira, smoky chorizo, tender flank steaks seared over flame. Servers carried platters of roasted vegetables, bright salads with tomatoes and onions slicked with olive oil, and piles of golden papas al rescoldo, potatoes cooked in the ashes.

As the evening deepened, Chef Patricio— "Pato" to his friends—raised a glass, his face flushed from the fire. "This," he declared, "is how we celebrate love in Argentina—smoke, meat, and joy!"

Everyone lifted their glasses. The scene was loud, generous, almost chaotic, and absolutely perfect.

Suddenly, someone in the back by one of the brand-new barns shouted, "Fire!"

At first, no one reacted. The party was still in full swing, glasses clinking, laughter rolling across the courtyard, the music carrying above it all. The warning seemed swallowed by the noise.

Then came another shout—louder, sharper. "Everyone out! There's a fire… huge fire coming this way!"

Heads whipped around. Beyond the glow of the string lights, orange sparks swirled in the wind. A curtain of flame leapt into view, driven hard by gusts that bent the olive trees and sent patio umbrellas, name tags, and even chairs tumbling across the lawn. In seconds, the air filled with smoke and flying embers, choking out the laughter, replacing it with screams.

Panic rippled through the crowd. Guests abandoned tables, kicking over chairs as they bolted. Parents scooped up children, others clutched shoes or jackets against the whipping wind. A line of bridesmaids tried to guide guests toward the vineyard slope, but the gale scattered them, voices snatched away before they could finish their sentences.

"Call 911!" someone shouted into the chaos. Finn, scanning the crowd for Melissa, pulled out his phone, called 911, and shouted the address into the receiver, one ear pressed tight to block the roar of wind, flame, and panicked voices. The operator replied calmly, "Someone already called, sir. Police and firefighters are on their way."

Thankfully she found him and they started guiding the scared guests down the hill where the road was. The fire moved with terrifying speed, tearing across the barns and racing for the venue, the wind stroking the blaze. Guests stumbled down through the vines toward the road, their silhouettes flickering in the hellish glow. Smoke clawed at their throats; sparks stung their faces. Couples held on to each other, running blind through the rows.

Sirens wailed in the distance, faint at first, then growing, answering the desperate calls. Fire trucks roared up the road, lights cutting through the smoke. Firefighters spilled out, barking orders, their figures disappearing into the haze as hoses uncoiled and the first blasts of water arced against the flames. Moments later, the streams began to push the fire back.

"John was still in a daze but relieved. The paramedics had patched him up, and the fire chief assured him that everyone was safe and unharmed. Now he sat on the ground against a massive oak tree, and beside him, half-buried in ash, rested the magnum of La Tâche he had nearly died saving."

The two employees sat in silence, joined quickly by dozens more survivors, all of them frozen in shock. Juliet's wedding dress still smoldered, ruined beyond repair, though she didn't care. Her face was weary as her eyes darted desperately, searching near and far. Her mom, Laura rushed over, Jason right behind her. 'Are you okay, Juliet?' her mother asked as she embraced her tightly. Juliet pulled away, saying hurriedly, 'I'm fine, Mom,' before turning back around.

'Paul!' She had already cried out again and again, her voice ragged. Summoning the last of her breath, she screamed once more into the choking smoke: 'Paul, where are you? Has anyone seen Paul?"

At last, he emerged, running through the thick orange haze, only twenty-five feet away but nearly invisible. "I'm here, love! I see you!" Paul shouted, stumbling forward.

He sprinted across the road toward her, arms outstretched, when suddenly a convoy of firetrucks roared through, sirens screaming, horns blaring. Juliet gasped as Mike lunged forward, pulling Paul back just in time. The trucks thundered past, nearly mowing him down.

For what felt like interminable minutes, Juliet stood frozen, peering between the trucks, hoping they would pass so Paul could reach her. At last, the convoy disappeared as quickly as it had come, and Paul broke through the smoke into her arms. She clung to him as if she'd never let go again.

Mike joined them, embracing them both with a shaky laugh. "Well, we'll never forget this wedding, you two."

Paul exhaled, managing a grin despite the chaos. "No chance we're doing this again, and no vow renewal, either!"

Mike went to sit next to his friend John, picked up the bottle, gave him a gentle pat on the back, and said with a perplexed look, "Really? You had this bottle in your cellar the whole time and didn't share? Someone told me you risked your life to save it—that was fucking dumb!"

John replied in a soft voice, "I was going to open it tonight."

"Next time, if you're going to run back into a fire," Mike said with a sarcastic edge, "make sure you grab that great bottle of Plinth Cab I got you."

They both laughed softly. John's expression shifted, solemn and teary. "It's all gone."

"Not Frank Gehry's work," Mike said, pointing through the smoke that had finally begun to clear. Most of the wooden structures were heavily damaged, but the titanium-roofed architectural wonder still stood strong.

They rose together, embraced, and in a rush of relief and exhaustion, laughter and a dance of joy followed. "Fuck it," John exclaimed, "I'll rebuild that bad larry. It's only money!" He pulled a wine key from his pocket, cut the foil, and popped the cork. He held the bottle to his nose, exaggerated the sniff, and winked, "Smokey."

Mike snorted at the joke, the air around them was still thick with smoke. John took a sip, then passed the bottle along.

Paul said, "Madame Monier, would you do us the honor?" Juliet squinted after her sip, lips puckered. "Not sure about that one," she admitted, older wines were never her thing. Mike finally chimed in, "This wine is unreal. I can't believe it's still got fruit—earthy, nutty, and mushroomy. Wow!"

"Give me that shit," said Jason as he gulped what seemed like half the bottle. "Fuck, that's good!" He checked the label. "1923 La Tâche. No wonder this pinot is so fucking spectacular!".

When it reached Paul, he took his sip slowly. The wine was exquisite, rich, layered, unforgettable. But in that surreal moment, even its perfection was secondary. He looked at Juliet, his new wife, and felt the truth settle deep inside him —all his dreams had come true.

He knew then he was ready to step into his future, accepting the role of Managing Partner and winemaking director at Gentleman Farmer Estate, working side by side with his new father-in-law.

Thank you for taking this journey with me,

and spending your time with my words.

Until we meet again — The End.

ACKNOWLEDGMENTS

This book would not have been written without the wonderful people in my life. I have been fortunate to know many who helped shape Napa Valley into what it is today: visionaries, craftsmen, and characters whose influence continues to define this extraordinary place. Some have left indelible marks that everyone can see. Others have contributed in quieter, more subtle ways, known only to those close enough to witness their impact.

Above all, I wish to express my heartfelt gratitude to all who inspired me, directly or indirectly, to write this book. Your spirit, kindness, and creativity have colored the canvas of my life. If you find your reflection in these pages, by name or by guise, know it was painted with gratitude and love.

I am especially grateful to my daughters, Manon and Juliette, to my wife, Melissa, and to my brothers and close friends, including Larry, Rex, Marsha, and Anita, whose infinite patience and kind support carried me through this creative journey.

The question I've been asked most often since writing my memoir, Butcher of American Idioms, has been, "Am I in your book?" My reply has always been the same: you won't know unless you read it and take this journey with me. So please, spend some time with my words, and perhaps you'll find your name among them.

To satisfy my friends, mentors, family, collaborators, and supporters, the community leaders, activists, makers and shapers, and the many unsung heroes who give this valley its heart, and with a wink, here is a list of those who have meant so much to me over the past thirty years in Napa Valley. I could never include everyone, but I've tried my best.

Abramovitch, Itamar. Aguilar Olea, Oscar. Albrecht, Brent and Laura. Allen, Julia. Allen, Nick. Ammons, Marie-Laure. Anderson, Kale. Arns, Bob and Ann. Ashworth, Chris and Veronica. Aurilia, Rich. Axelson, Kurtis. Baccino, Tim. Balik, Allen. Barrios, Blake. Barstad, Guy. Barry, Dick and Christine. Belz, Patrick. Bennett, Walter and Diana.Bernards, Ken and Teresa. Bernstein, Len and Annette Cross. Bevan, Russell. Bias, Chris and Patty. Bischof, Tim and Cheryl. Bishofberger, Diane. Black, Mike and Carol. Blanchard, Chris. Blicker, Stefan and Joanne. Boell, Ed and Georgette. Boldrini, Massi and Jennifer. Boon, Hunter. Boyd, Stan and Joan. Brady, Amanda. Breiman, Roy. Brocamontes, Tom. Brune, Mark and Alison. Buck, Tom. Bull, James. Burgess, Colin. Burkett, James and Allison. Butler, Earl and Ann Evanston. Caldwell, John and Joy. Carlisle, Lorenzo and Marrissa. Carmichael, Chris. Carpenter, Chris and Tina. Carter, Sarah. Case, Amy, Ed and Margie. Castiglioni, Marsha. Cavanaugh, Bob. Cavanaugh, Nick and Kim. Ceja, Amelia and Pedro. Chang, Flora. Clark, Tara and Spencer. Clark, Tom and Laurie. Coffy, Marshall and Karen. Corona, Fred. Cornu, Michel. Cortez, Carmen. Cross, Rob and Shannon. Cuddy, Stephen. Cunningham, Lonnie. Dahlberg, Eric and Michele. Dappen, Duane.

Davis, Charles and Ann. Davis, Ted (Airstream). Dawson, Dan and Holly. De Boer, Jeffrey and Roberta. De Moraes, Alex and Juanita. DeSimone, Mike and Jeff Jenssen. Delpuech, Genevieve. Difilippo, John. Dinkel, Tom and Marcie. Distler, Steve. Doidge, John and Judy. Doody, Brian and Laura Larson. Doran, Jeff. Dulal, Krishna. Economides, Antonia. Edwards, Mark and Gretchen. Ellman, Neil and Lance. Enfield, Mike and Cathy. Eppich, Julie. Erasmy, Kim. Erasmy, Lois and Joe. Erickson, Andy. Fayard, Julien. Ferdon, Vivian Ritondale. Ficeli, Dave and Christi. Finkelstein, Judd and Holly. Filippini, Joe. Fischer, Joe. Fisher, LeeAnne. Flanagan, Eric and Kit. Fourmeaux, Jean-Noel. Fournier, Marc. Franson, Paul. Frappia, Bob and Theresa. Friedes, Michael. Frias brothers. Gaffney, Phil and Laura. Gafner, Mel and Rosemary. Gansky, Lisa. Garry, Vincent. Genoshe, Mike. Gibbs, Lisa. Gladfelter, Jim. Goad, Dwight and Diana. Gomez-España, Javier and Marie. Goodwin, Evelyn. Goorjian, Michael. Graham, Mike and Teresa. Grange, Frank and Linda. Green, Don and Marisa. Green, John. Gregory, Katrina. Gregory, Ryan. Griffin, Jim and Donna. Griffin, Rebecca Sciandri. Gromacki, Kristine and Tod Ratfield. Guerrera, Gio and Marie Dolcini. Gustin, Bob. Hadeler, Marcia and Michael. Halpert, Fred. Hamilton, Kathie. Hannaford,

John. Hansen, Linda. Hansens, Sarah and Chris. Hagopian, Harout and Marie. Harris, Susan. Harrison, Neal. Hatton, Ryan. Heine, Mike and Tammy. Hernandez, Ramona and Umar, Anna. Herrera, Rolando and Lorena. Hersly, Adam and Stacy. Hertelendy, Ralph. Hewitt, Jennifer. Higuera, Michael and Laurie. Hill, Ryan. Hirschmann, Peter and Karen. Hoefliger, Jean and Chelsea. Holcomb, Michael. Hoopes, Miten and Lindsay. Huether, Gordon and Darcy. Hurley, Greg and Nicole. Hyatt, Brett and Kelly. Jacobsen, Peter and Gween. Jasso, Efrain and Cathy. Jeffries, Pat and Christie. Jessup, Craig and Susan. Johnson, Chuck and Ledene. Johnson, Jason. Johnson, Michael. Johnston, Mike. Jones, Dawn Simpson. Jones, Jennifer. Kalulu, Choolwe. Kauffman, Vaughn. Keebler, Kent. Keffer, Eric and Heather. Kennedy, Jenna. Kearney, Dave and Elaine. Keplinger, DJ and Helen. Kettering-Peck, Dennis and Brenda. Kincanon, Jerry and Pam. Kirby, David. Knight, Sean. Knoth, Ryan and Nicole. Koschitzky, Maayan and Dana. Kreer, Kina. Lail, Robin. Laliberte, Bill and Jennifer. Langner, Philip. Lasker, Dave. Lauwers, Marc and Beth Rypins. Lawler, Tony and Lisa. Lawler, David and Catherine. Lessler, Mark. Leslie-Stewart, Doug and Robin. Lohin, David and Anita. Lopez, Maria. Loustau, Didier. Lubash, Tod and Cherie. Luros, Mary. Mancini, Max and

Kathy. Manzares, Jenelle. Marcencia, Will and Julissa. Marnell, Pat and Melissa. Martin, Monte. Martin, Tim. Mason, Ben. Matthiasson, Steve. McCall, Manon and Kyle. McCall, Steve and Jenny. McClenahan, Bob. McGill, Craig. McPherson, Jay. Meeks, Doug. Mejia, Jose. Melka, Philippe and Cherie. Mensonides, Kristin and Joel. Merkley, Patrick. Meyerowitz, Ron. Miller, Charles. Miller, Lee. Mink, Bill and Angela. Montoya, Macario. Moody, Marc. Moore, Jason and Angelica. Morlet, Luc. Morrow Mapes, Ilse. Moses-Hall, Ann and James. Murphy, Annie (Mom). Murphy, Brendan and Catherine. Murphy, Juliette. Cathy O'Sullivan. Mercier, Eric and Annie. Murphy, Jason and Carola. Rex Pickett and Joy Murphy. Murphy, Kieran and Aimee. *Murphy, Melissa, my beloved wife*. Murphy, Niall and Kieko. Narvaez, Bernie Alfredo. Neumann, Tim. Nuss, Tyler, Timmy, Lori and Brian. O'Connor, Kevin and Nicole. Odegard, Philip. Olsen, Martin and Jeni. Pack, Sean. Parker, Bill and Juanita. Parrott, Gerry. Parr, Claire. Patel, Raj. Patz, Donald. Peel, Bob and Kris. Pepin, Jacques. Perry, Mike and Sheila. Person, Daniel and Jacqueline. Phillips, Jim and Beth. Phairas, Debra. Piombo, Tony. Pierret, Joe and Monica. Policy, Carmen and Gail. Powers, Stan and Sandra. Provost, Dave and Roxanne. Pramuk, Sean.

Przybylinsky, Pete and Erin. Purdy, Mark. Quast, Michael and Kathy. Ramirez, Art. Ramirez, Francisco. Rasmussen, David and Rhoni. Ray, Jason and Laura. Rea, Steven. Regan, Matthew and Lindsey. Rein, Daniel and Brittany. Renda, Andy. Renteria, Oscar and Denise. Richardson, Gary and Rosemary. Rigo, Pascal. Robicheau, Brenda. Robins, Brett. Robledo, Vanessa. Rolland, Michel. Rom, Lisa. Rouas, Bettina. Roulin, Aurelien. Roy, Shirley. Salyer, Mick. Sanders, Dana and Dynie. Sanchez, Kathy. Schilter, John. Schluns, Leonard and Kim. Schwartz, John and Carrie. Sedeno, Dave and Carole. Sedgley, Scott. Seay, James and Ann. Senkow, Dan. Shanker, Gopal and Seena. Shindle, Don. Showket, Kal and Dorothy. Silva, Bob and Katherine. Silverthorn, Iain. Simpson, Julie. Smith, Craig. Smith, Mark and Kristy. Smith, Nate. Tolbert, Sonia. Stevens, Monica. Stevens, Susan. Strohl, Curtis. Sturtz, Anthony and Linda. Surh, Don and Shelley. Sumpter, Cameron. Sutton, Andy. Tannhauser, Sylvie. Tavakoli, Kian and Erika. Teague, Kevin and Taylor. Tessier, Philip. Tessler, Bob and Carol. Thompson, David. Tocchini, Corey and Keyo. Torres, Gloria. Trevarthen, Toby and Debbie. Tsai, Larry and Mary-Ann. Umutyan, Dr Ari. Uran, Josh. Uytengsu, Michael and Tara. Valencia, Israel. VanHoutan, Lessly. Ventrello, Faith and Steve. Verdis, Verdis and

Gina. Villasenor, Carlos. Von Sahl, Richard. Warson, Paul and Leah. Ware, Cotton. Waugh, Ryan and Crystal. Weir, Irit. Weirich, Bill and Helen. Wendel, Chris and Hillary. Whitney, Craig and Melissa. White, Doug. Wiegard, Mark. Williams, Craig. Woolery, Elijah and Courtney. Wright, Will. Wu, Phong. Yataco, Martin. Youngman, Larry and Pam. Youngman, Samantha. Zupon, Bryan.

About the Author

An author and seasoned entrepreneur, he is also a photographer, painter, foodie, and wine aficionado; a mentor, a Kenpo black belt, and above all, a proud papa. Learn more in his memoir, Butcher of American Idioms.

www.ingramcontent.com/pod-product-compliance
Lightning Source LLC
Chambersburg PA
CBHW030758200726
PP18592100001B/3